FATIGUE ANALYSIS OF A PAPER AIRPLANE

Michael R. Urban, Ph.D.

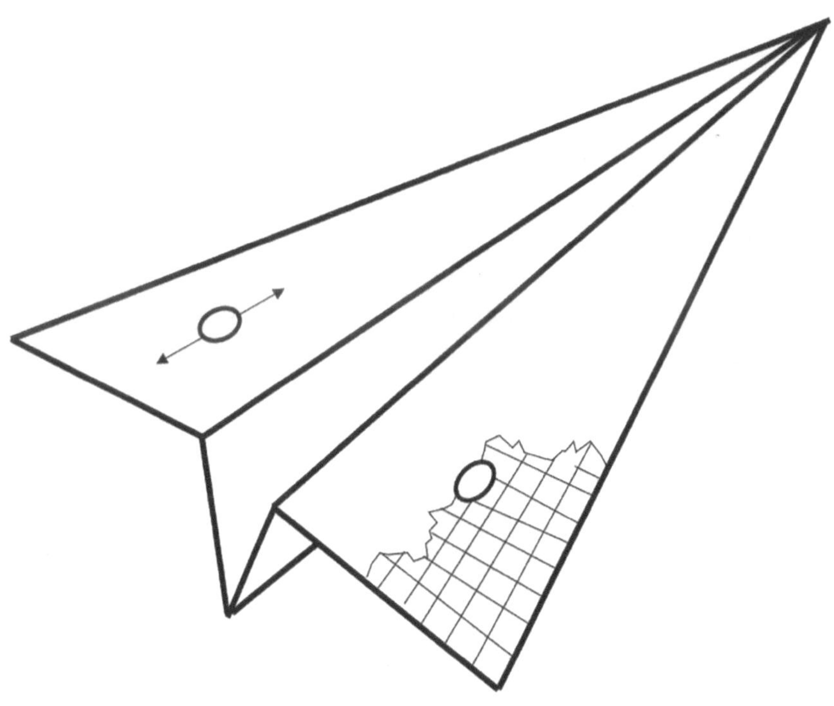

Class Notes

ISBN 979-8-88851-419-1 (Paperback)
ISBN 979-8-88851-420-7 (Digital)

Covenant Books
11661 Hwy 707
Murrells Inlet, SC 29576
www.covenantbooks.com

To my family. They have always been such a huge supporter of my writing and encouraged me to never give up on my dreams. They gave me my greatest title: Dad.

TTFN

Aircraft can be developed with powerful computing power or with a simple paper and pencil. While it is never recommended to completely neglect the capabilities offered by current and future computing, the use of pencil and paper is highly endorsed.

Computing abilities will never be a substitute for human imagination and creativity. One should always ask themselves, would you be thrilled or terrified if the use of computing was lost?

A paper airplane developed by combining paper, pencil, and expertise will be cost-efficient and superior to one born purely from application of extensive computer power.

CONTENTS

Chapter 1:   Introduction 1

   1.0 Introduction 1

   1.1 Fatigue Analysis 1

   1.2 Cyclic Damage 3

   1.2.1 Stress-Life 4

   1.2.2 Strain Life 7

   1.2.3 Fracture Mechanics 7

   1.2.4 Analysis Methods Conclusion 8

   1.3 Summary 9

Chapter 2:   Stress-Life 11

   2.0 S-N Curves 11

   2.1 Expanded Knowledge: Stress-Life Curves/Surfaces 13

   2.1.1 Analysis: High-Cycle Horizons 16

   2.1.2 Analysis: Low-Cycle Plastic Behavior 18

   2.1.3 Summary: Stress-Life Curve Adjustments 20

   2.3 Curve Shapes 20

   2.4 Surfaces 25

   2.5 Type of Calculation 27

   2.5.1 New Product Curves 28

   2.5.2 Field Support Curves 31

   2.5.3 Stress-Life Curve Summary 34

   2.6 Scatter-Needed Line and Surface 35

   2.7 Conclusion 38

Chapter 3:   Energy Methods 41

   3.0 Energy-Life Methods 41

   3.1 Analysis Evolution 41

   3.1.1 Cyclic Damage Normalizing Factor 42

   3.1.2 Adjustment Factors 44

3.1.3 Complex Loadings 46
3.1.4 Control 48
3.1.5 Fracture Mechanics 49
3.1.6 Expanding Horizons..50
3.2 Finite Element and Stress-Life 53
3.3 Selecting Test Data 54
3.4 Energy Reduces Complication...56
3.4.1 The Universal Scalar 56
3.4.2 Neuber and Peterson Factors 58
3.4.3 Distance-Scaling Factor 60
3.4.4 Converting Stress Field to an Energy Scalar 61
3.4.5 2D Surface—3D Volume 64
3.5 Round Hole Example 65
3.6 Conclusion 77
Chapter 4:   Unification...80
4.0 Uniting Fracture Mechanics and Stress-Life.......................80
4.1 Uniting Methodologies 80
4.2 Fracture Mechanic...83
4.3 Classical Stress-Life..86
4.4 Unite with New Curves 87
4.5 Focus on the Physics and the Possible...............................88
4.6 Conclusion 91
Chapter 5:   Test Results 94
5.0 Uniting Analysis with Test Results.....................................94
5.1 Test Data Application..94
5.2 Energy-Life 96
5.3 Fracture Mechanics 99
5.4 Test Data..101
5.5 Define Scatter 102
5.6 Conclusion..103

References 105

CHAPTER 1

Introduction

Fatigue Analysis

1.0 Introduction

Structural fatigue analysis is the assessment of cyclic loads on structural components. The use of the word *fatigue* in the analysis originated in the nineteenth century. It is based on an explanation that, like with living things, structural components simply got tired or fatigued. This is a gross oversimplification of the process. There was no clear understanding of the physics, so a general *fatigue* explanation was all that could be applied.

Now, almost two centuries later, there is a tremendous volume of research, theories, and test data. The years of work have made great progress in understanding the fatigue phenomena. Unfortunately, there is still a great deal of ambiguity in the process.

This text summarizes the current state of fatigue analysis and presents methods that combine existing knowledge and current technology toward a reduction in the level of ambiguity.

1.1 Fatigue Analysis

This book is about suggestions and guidance, not basic fatigue theory. The number of fatigue papers and books that have already been published are too numerous to count. The primary point of this book is to stress that a physical configuration is not dependent on an analysis; in fact, it's just the opposite.

The goal of any analysis is to add a level of knowledge that can be useful in improving the reliability, effective ness, and safety of any physical component. Do not let the calculation itself be the reason for the work. A calculation on its own can never alter the actual outcome; it can, at best, predict the results.

Fatigue performance predictions can be highly important, but do not let calculations themselves be the objective. To be most effective, a calculation needs to have a purpose and a reasonable objective. Is the analysis supporting a fielded component, possibly an inspection requirement? Is the analysis part of a detailed laboratory experiment? What level of scatter is expected? The requirements must be known (see figure1.1).

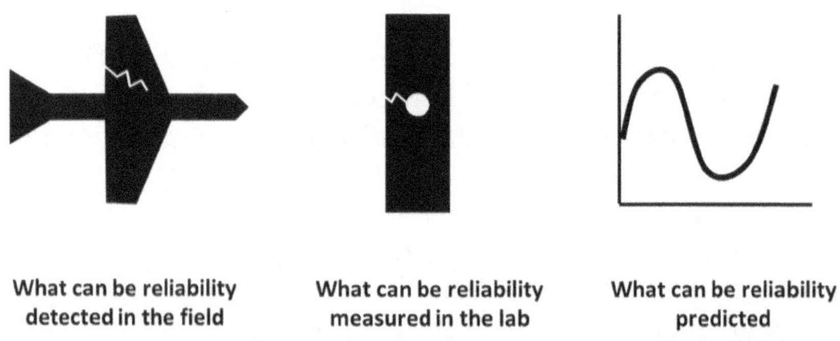

Figure 1.1 What can be done?

Computers are a great asset. They present opportunities that were, a short time ago, impossible. It is certain computers and the opportunities they present will continue to expand. Analysis needs to advance hand in hand with capabilities.

Computers can also obscure an analysis' Achilles' heel. Avoid falling prey to accepting a prediction merely because it was generated on a computer. The user needs to be able to perform the analysis work without a Graphical User Interface (GUI) and must fully understand the physics and limitations. It can be very useful to use pencil-and-paper hand calculations to verify or bracket a prediction to help understand the computer's output.

1.2 Cyclic Damage

Damage from cyclic loading has long been a concern, especially for metallic components. The repeated loading to levels, which may be significantly below a material's ultimate capability, or even yield points, can eventually cause failures.

The term fatigue refers to getting tired after prolonged periods of exertion. The term was carried over in describing the breakdown and failure of structural components after repeated loadings. The terminology is accurate in describing how items breakdown after repeated events. It should be inaccurate in portraying the fatigue analysis process. A process which fatigues the user will eventually fail to achieve its objective.

For most details, the majority of the cyclic loads are required to establish of-nucleate damage. This means that the largest portion of the damaging cycles occur when the inspection is impractical. It also puts the majority of the damaging cycles at a size where continuum mechanic cannot be used for highly localized stresses. Figure 1.2 illustrates the situation with analyzing and monitoring progressing cyclic damage under load control parameters.

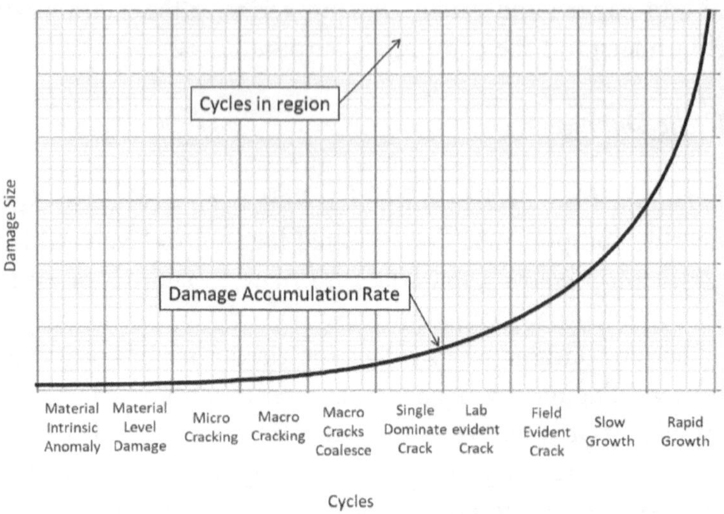

Figure 1.2 Zones of crack growth rates.

Many mathematical formulations have been employed over the years to help predict cyclic loading performance with the goal of understanding and, ultimately, preventing failure. Fatigue analysis is relatively new when compared to static loading analysis. Predictive techniques for understanding static failures have been successfully used for many years. It is thereby understandable that their techniques were extending into fatigue analysis. The key question is, Was it optimal to expand static techniques to cyclic loading analyses?

1.2.1 Stress-Life

Stress was, and remains, highly popular in representing the internal loading condition within a continuum. The load per unit area factor correlates well with many fielded static components, as well as laboratory test data.

Static and cyclic analyses become more complicated when plastic yielding occurs. Plasticity introduces history effects. To prevent the complication of history effects and prevent overloading, most components are designed to keep structural internal loads below the material's yield point. Keeping loading below yield points allows for linear elastic calculations. This text focuses solely on linear elastic cycling.

Early on, the use of stress with added factors was adapted for modeling the number of cycles to failure. Stress was adopted as the preferred representation of a material's fatigue performance. Adapting stress for cyclic loading made unifying static and fatigue calculations straightforward. The technique allows fatigue predictions to converge with static failure at a single or partial loading cycle, as depicted in figure 1.3.

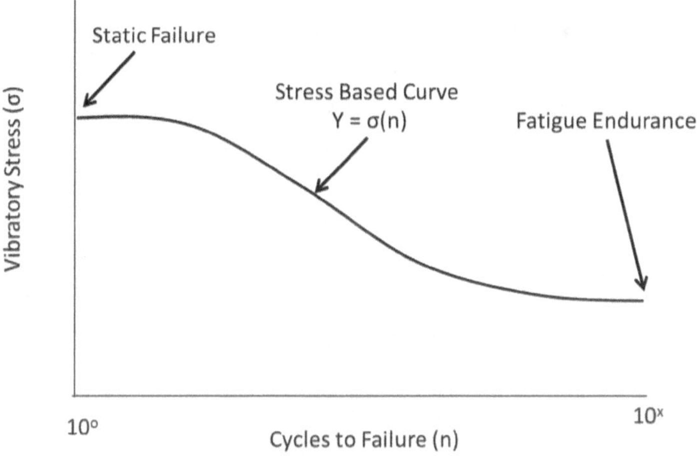

Figure 1.3 Single loading to failure connected to endurance.

The method, now commonly referred to as stress-life, proved to be a straightforward technique for representing fatigue performance. At a high level, using stress looks to be a simple solution. Unfortunately, there is some level of debate as to what stress component to employ in the analysis. The three primary stresses candidates use are: gross section stress, net section stress, or average stress (shown in figure 1.4).

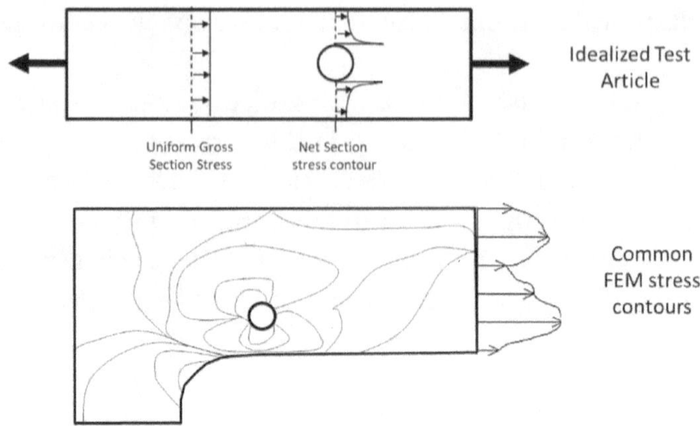

Figure 1.4 Net and gross section stress average (FEM versus idealized).

In many simple geometries used in test articles, gross and net section stresses can be easily and clearly determined. Based on testing, it was found that net section stress correlated best. Net section is the most common stress utilized in stress-life analysis, even today. Unfortunately, net section stress is often not determined straightforwardly by most finite element models used in design. Alternatively, an average stress is used for Finite Element Method (FEM) in lieu of true net section stress. As is shown in figure 1.4, the simple stress distributions of a common center hole specimen is far less complex than the example, FEM contour plot, which is common in product-design support.

Issues quickly arose with stress-life predictions. The peak net section stress proved to not be a good predictor of performance. Peak stress did not correlate well across a variety of geometries. The high local peak stress skewed predictions.

Experimental data shows that the larger the volume of highly stressed material, the lower the fatigue lives are for a given stress level. Stressed volume is an empirical factor that attempts to adjust for this amount of highly stressed material.

In general, stressed volume is straightforward. A very tiny hole will behave much like a uniformly stressed item of equal size using a far-field stress level. A large hole will behave similar to a uniformly stressed article but at the peak stress. In detailed applications, the "highly" stressed volume is not easily determined and often relies on subjective inputs.

Eventually, the straightforward stress-life method relies on an empirical adjusted stress concentration combined with numerous other highly suspect adjustments. The factors all proved to be difficult to represent, resulting in many highly empirical and subjective factors being introduced.

1.2.2 Strain Life

An alternative to stress-life was introduced to help objectify the fatigue predictive process. Strain life would use peak loading to represent fatigue performance. As the name implies, *strain* is used as the defining loading factor. Strain life is presented as not having the limitations of yield, unlike stress-life. It could also represent history effects, which are commonly understood to be of paramount importance once yielding has occurred. While the promise of strain life was to objectify the analysis inputs, it, too, started to fall victim to subjective inputs.

1.2.3 Fracture Mechanics

Fracture mechanics was introduced to reduce the subjectivity of inputs. The technique would use the hard science of crack growth to represent fatigue behavior. After all, it is cracks that ultimately cause fatigue failures. While a very noble undertaking, fracture mechanics also fell prey to subjective inputs. It was found that in many situations, the majority of cycles were applied, while the crack lengths were small compared to the metallic grain structures. The material was not homogeneous at that point of the crack growth. Continuum mechanics criteria, which are vital to the analysis, had fallen apart. Pure science was replaced with a new set of assumptions and subjective inputs required to match test results.

Fracture mechanics has the ability to not just predict total cycles to failure but to predict the size of a crack throughout its growth cycle. If the crack size predictive portion of the analysis is discarded as imprecise, then what is the benefit over stress-life or strain life? Does fracture mechanics become an extension of stress-life once lacking crack size versus cycles?

Some texts have proposed using a single factor for adjusting fracture mechanics predictions. It has been postulated that an arbitrary initial crack size is all that is required. The initial crack size is allowed to vary, wherever it may need to go. It is not completely frank to show fracture mechanics having only one factor, such as initial flaw size while describing stress-life as having numerous factors. If the test data shows the factors used in stress-life truly do impact cyclic life, then how can they be neglected in any methodology?

In most cases, the numerous factors from stress-life are included in fracture mechanics. The hidden initial step in fracture mechanics employs a calculation where all the same stress-life factors are combined to produce the single input adjustment called an initial crack size. This fracture mechanics technique is merely a sleight of hand. Initial crack size merely incorporates numerous adjustments.

True fracture mechanics with true single crack growth is a powerful tool. It is less useful once crack length data is not predictable. Fracture mechanics should not obscure subjective factors by employing initial crack techniques. Initial crack sizes are often so small that they invalidate continuum assumptions.

1.2.4 Analysis Methods Conclusion

Stress-life, strain life, and fracture mechanics are all excellent methods; it's just that they all have limitations. Applying them when they are most accurate will greatly help the precision of the predictions. The common denominator is physics. You have to understand the physics of the individual situation and what knowledge is desired from the calculation.

It is the author's opinion that some level of subjectivity is needed with all current techniques. It may be that fatigue predictions are subject to a level of chaos that prevents some configurations from ever being precisely predicted. This is not to say no knowledge can be gained through analysis. The point is that limits must be acknowledged and held.

In fatigue analysis, assumptions matter, and often they are the most important item. Too often the determination of internal stress is given paramount importance. It is agreed that accurate stress is of high importance. It is also understood but often neglected that analysis adjustment factors are just as important. Many of these factors have significant limitations that need to be understood.

The best way to conduct an analysis is to use all available knowledge and assets. Combine them in a unified approach through holistic and realistic methods to produce the highest quality predictions. It is the accumulation of all analysis inputs that produces the highest quality fatigue prediction. Therefore, all inputs must be given equal weighing.

It is easy to tout an analysis' strong points. What is more critical is to point out its limitations. Do not be overly negative, but be honest. It is helpful to know why an analysis path was taken. It is important to fully describe what was avoided and issues which could limit the precision of a prediction. Do not only list an analysis' strong points.

1.3 Summary

The purpose of this text it to point out the great things that can be accomplished with current tools, and also to expand the requirements for reporting fatigue predictions. By reducing (not eliminating) subjective inputs and expanding physics-based inputs, the consistency and accuracy of fatigue predictions can both be greatly enhanced.

Unifying test results through physics, applying appropriate analysis methods, and optimizing computing capacities can improve the fatigue predictive process. Unification of all the analysis steps will add consistency to the analysis process.

Like with any process, a fatigue analysis must be brought under control before it can be improved. Manufacturing has long understood the benefits of a controlled process. The issue with most fatigue processes is that they must maintain enough freedom to allow design optimization while simultaneously maintaining control. This produces a difficult yet important conundrum.

Many fatigue calculations are merely a mix of black magic, three-card Monte, smoke and mirrors, and a dash of science. The "science" presented to sell estimates may be little more than guesses. Unsuspecting managers may fall victim to oversold predictions. That is not to say that there are not many highly useful fatigue calculations; the point is, there are many times when theory is pushed far beyond its ability while hiding behind an awesome-looking GUI. Often only trends are predictable. The trends can be highly useful. They start to lose credibility when the trend is passed off as a precise calculation.

It is fairly obvious that increasing stress of a given geometry or increasing a local peaking for a given applied load will both reduce predicted cycles to failure. Using a material with greater cyclic loading capability will increase fatigue live predictions. Lowering cyclic loads will increase cyclic loading predictions. While all are very obvious, none are hard cyclic loading predictions. Always be fully aware of what is being calculated.

The best analysis is a holistic analysis. Holistic analysis, along with complete answers, is invaluable in designing and maintaining safe and efficient structures.

Sometimes the correct answer is there is no prediction which can account for the given inputs and produce an answer with acceptable accuracy. Maybe good, better, and best is all that can be determined alone with some limiting values.

The key takeaway is to always question and never fool yourself. Fatigue methods offer great opportunities to improve systems. Apply methods when they are most useful and use the greatest caution when attempting to expand established limits.

CHAPTER 2

Stress-Life

Formulation and Limitation of Linear Elastic Fatigue Behavior

2.0 S-N Curves

There are countless books and publications on classic stress-life analysis methods. The purpose of this chapter is to point out possible improvements and general limitations of the theory. Limitations are too often hidden in automated routines. It is important to fully understand the limitations and start a conversation on when and how best to use powerful stress-life analysis tools.

Stress-life is a powerful tool when used in its applicable region. A concern with some analyses is the application of the technique where it doesn't fully apply. A brief summary of the possible pitfalls of stress-life can be very helpful in developing a useful and highly accurate methodology. One of the primary pitfalls of stress-life is its use in plastic regions and near-singular regions. Entering either of these two regions, while tempting, needs to be avoided.

Never ignore knowledge you have or infer knowledge you don't have. As obvious as this statement appears, it is all too often not applied in fatigue analyses. Many fatigue analyses reports predicted failures to greater precision than their calculations bear out. Inferring implied data accuracy, which is not actually known, is often to blame. Error and scatter can also be introduced when applying theories where they no longer hold merely for the convenience of generating predictions. Credibility of predictions is further undermined by ignoring the numerous erroneous predictions while touting the few successes.

One major item that is often glossed over is the use of a near-singular region on the stress-life curve. A very clever technique for presenting a stress-life curve is to plot the stress-versus-cycles curve rotated ninety degrees from how it is primarily applied in practice (figure 2.1). Through this presentation method, August Wohler (1870) was able to depict a convergence to an endurance life rather than a singularity to an endurance stress.

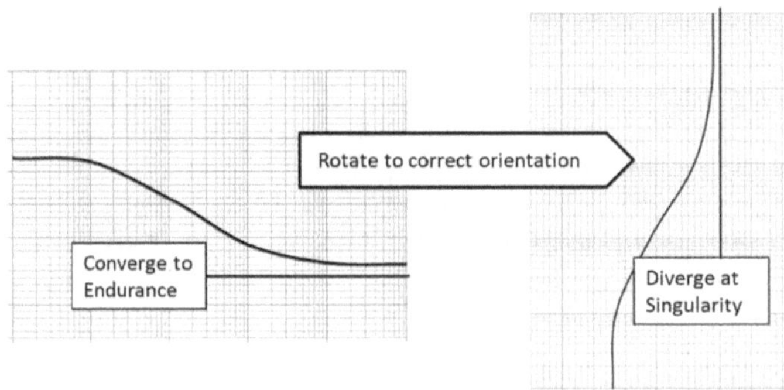

Figure 2.1 Curve orientation.

All analyses must acknowledge the limitations of the current state of the technology and, even more importantly, the physics of the configuration. In the lower-stress, higher-cycle region of classic stress-life behavior, there is a singularity when attempting to determine life as a dependent variable based on stress as the independent variable. The singularity causes a breakdown in classic stress-life theory of fatigue behavior at endurance

2.1 Expanded Knowledge: Stress-Life Curves/Surfaces

Stress-life curves have long focused on relating cyclic loads with cycles to failure. One question is, how is failure defined? More on this topic later. While this simple relationship is the very foundation of stress-life methods, it is not the whole picture. Excessive focus on this relationship has often obscured other factors. A much more holistic approach using all available information and tools is recommended.

The representation of stress-life allowable cyclic curves has not changed much over the many years since its introduction, yet the technology around those curves has evolved from pencil-and-paper approximations to computer simulations.

Producing the most accurate and informed fatigue predictions requires stress-life cyclic-allowable curves to be better integrated into current testing and analysis technologies. The capabilities of current systems should not be overly simplified in order to fit fatigue behavior representations which were optimized for bygone techniques.

One universal truth that does not change is to always apply all knowledge when attempting to solve a problem. Knowledge is the foundation of all fatigue analysis. It expands understanding but also puts limits on widely accepted standards. Accepting limits is difficult but necessary in producing and supporting efficient structures.

Loading rates are one example of knowledge which may not be fully utilized. When a high-frequency loading is applied along with a low-frequency loading, are they both of equal importance in the fatigue prediction? In a Miner's type linear cumulative damage summation, they are treated similarly. Both contribute a portion of the total damage. In actual designs, the physics of their impact may be completely different.

The issue is with the cycles required to accumulate damage. If the high frequency is orders of magnitude higher than the lower frequency and the high-frequency cycles are damaging, the number of cycles can overpower the lower frequencies' contribution to damage. The high cycle loading builds total cycles at an uncompromising pace. If any single high cycle contributes to fatigue, damage failure may happen quickly. If individual cycle caused no measurable damage, then the loading cycles are inconsequential. This sets up a step function similar to the situation depicted in figure 2.2. Clearly it will be beneficial to address loading rates as a key factor in damage accumulation calculations.

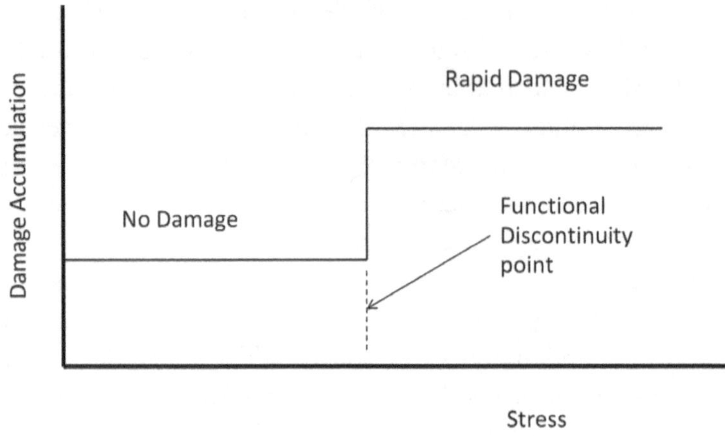

Figure 2.2 Fatigue damage set function.

Cyclic frequency loads in stress-life calculations can reside in four regions (figure 2.3). The first is in the higher stress region of the curve (OCF) where stresses can instantaneously produce damage.

Next is the linear cumulative damage region (LCF) where damage may incrementally accumulate. Most concerning for an analysis is cycling in the high-cycle zone (HCF) where usable predictions may become challenging, as scatter can play a significant role.

Finally is the loading zone where stresses should be non-damaging in an engineering sense (VFC), ideally producing no measurable damage. It would be highly beneficial to separate high and low-frequency loading when conducting fatigue analyses.

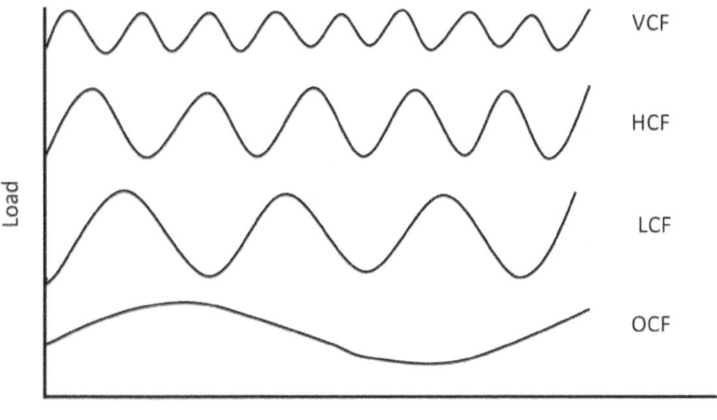

Figure 2.3 Cyclic loading rates.

There may also be cycles of high-stress plastic yielding. Extending linear elastic fatigue techniques into the plastic loading region has long been acknowledged as unacceptable. Stresses must remain linear elastic when linear elastic techniques are applied. If loading has history effects, then so will fatigue predictions. This requires stress-life cyclic-allowable curves be limited to the elastic stress region. This effort addresses the elastic portion of cyclic loading. It is highly recommended that new designs be developed to stay cyclically loading elastic.

Knowledge is also available in knowing what is being analyzed. Is the analysis aimed at new product development? Is the analysis reviewing the performance of a fielded component which experienced a failure? The focus may be with designing a test coupon. Knowing what is being analyzed is important in developing methods that are optimized for the given application. Using a holistic analysis is a superior method of gaining the best possible results.

Knowing cyclic rates, what is required of the analysis, what is being analyzed, and linear/plastic behavior are all important pieces of information which, when combined, will greatly enhance stress-life methods.

2.1.1 Analysis: High-Cycle Horizons

There are practical limits to stress-life predictive capacities. Stress-life curves become very flat near endurance in classical representation (figure 2.4). The flattening can become greater with the addition of steady stress. Often curves are only presented for low or no mean stress giving false assurance for usable cyclic curves at high R-ratios. Do not allow automated calculations to mask this important point.

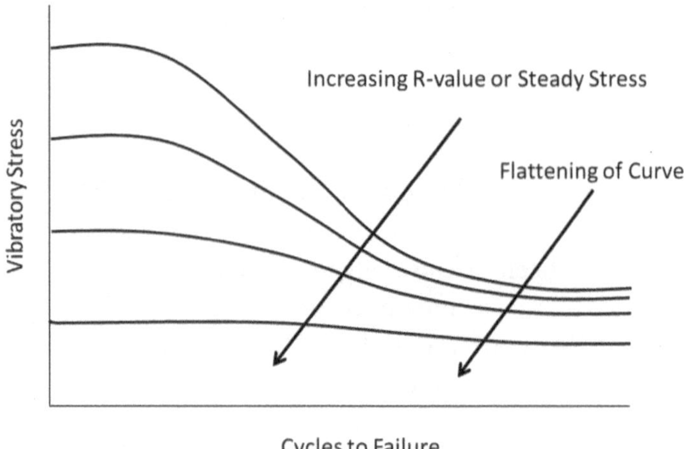

Figure 2.4 Stress-life curve flattening.

Like in cosmology where black holes cause a breakdown in physical laws, so will any singularity in any physical or mathematical scenario; the singularity in classical stress-life fatigue behavior is no exception.

While singularities are convenient mathematical tools that provide correlation curves relating regions leading up to the singularity, the singularity itself cannot exist in nature. This is where the mathematics and physics break down. The critical question is, how close to the singularity does the mathematical representation represent the true physics? And how close to the singularity can meaningful results be drawn?

The existence of a singularity infers an event horizon in the mathematics of fatigue, just like the ones around black holes. It is proposed that there is an event horizon in fatigue exactly like the horizon around black holes (figure 2.5).

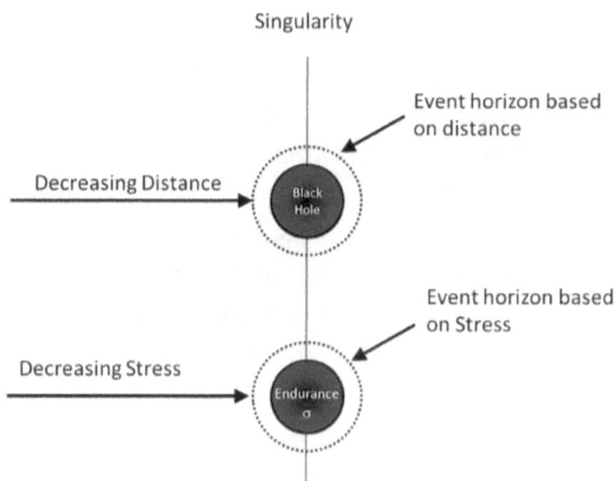

Figure 2.5 Singularity region.

The horizon is the point where the theory can no longer be applied. It is important to understand that applying theory where it does not apply can never produce practical results. Even a single pass over the event horizon will trigger a mathematical uncertainty that corrupts the entire calculation.

An important step in determining any limiting horizon is to find the point where uncontrollable variations in the inputs produce unacceptable variability in predictions, rendering those predictions worthless. This loss of acceptable stress-life accuracy will be reached before a total breakdown in the math-physics relationship. When results are no longer useful, a limit or horizon has been crossed. This event horizon in fatigue calculation should never be crossed because, as in the black hole analogy, there is no returning once the horizon has been crossed.

2.1.2 Analysis: Low-Cycle Plastic Behavior

As in the low-stress, high-cycle region, there is a practical limit in the high-stress, low-cycle region for classical stress-life linear elastic calculations. In the high-stress region, linear elastic representation may not apply.

Often the region where plasticity becomes a major factor can be approximated by relating two net section stress curves. The first curve is a smooth specimen, commonly referred to as a Kt = 1.0 curve. The second curve is for a notched specimen where there is a peak stress at a notch. This curve is commonly classified by a stress concentration value. Where the two curves significantly diverge can signify the onset of plastic-dominated behavior. An example is shown in figure 2.6. At approximately five thousand cycles, the two curves diverge. This indicates that for this situation, linear elastic calculations should not be applied if loading peak goes above the five-thousand-cycle stress level for the notched configuration. Strain life methods will have to be applied.

Applying linear elastic calculations is inviting, as it frees the user from the burden of tracking history effects which arise with plastic behavior or any behavior which causes permanent changes to the material. The simplicity of linear elastic calculations enticed many to hold to linear elastic theory too long. Like with the low-stress event horizon, there is a high-stress horizon for linear elastic behavior. Unlike at the low-stress horizon, there is a methodology to address the high-stress region. Strain life is one example of a method which fully accounts for history effects.

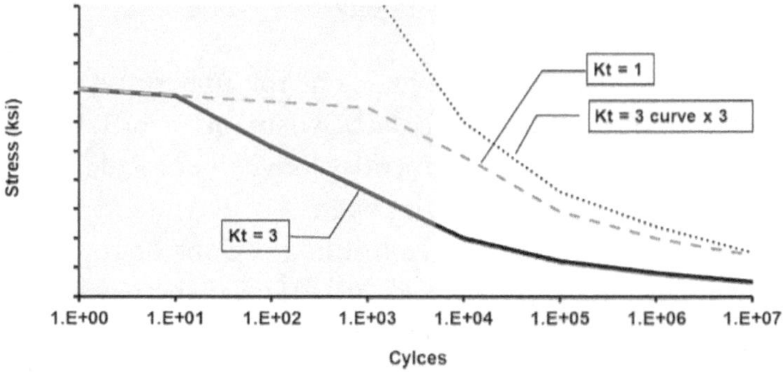

Figure 2.6 Plasticity limit approximation.

Using strain life in new design does require significant knowledge of future events. Predicting the future using history effects is a challenging task. It is only possible to predict a future outcome within a region of possible outcomes (Dowling). This complicates applying strain life for new product development. As in the lower-stress endurance region, uncontrollable scatter in inputs may produce unusable outputs. Strain life predicts a range of possible future outcomes, all of which will be influenced by the random occurrence of future events.

Strain life may be a more valuable tool in explaining past performance if the historical data has been properly collected. This makes strain life tools highly useful in investigating fatigue failures of highly loaded components. With loading history known, the application of plastic behavior becomes much more controllable.

The majority of new product designs will not require use of recurrent cyclic plasticity. Repeated plastic cycling is a rare need in new product design. A single plastic cycle, as in cold working, can often be satisfactorily analyzed using linear elastic analysis, but fatigue calculations under cyclic plasticity cannot be universally assessed using linear elastic methods. Plastic loading is a large topic to address for special applications. The scope of this work will therefore focus on the linear elastic region.

2.1.3 Summary: Stress-Life Curve Adjustments

Properly addressing the physics of the upper and lower event horizons for linear elastic fatigue behavior of metals significantly limits the region where linear theories like Miner's Rule are applicable. Miner touches on this in his paper.

Many users will hesitate in limiting regions of applicability of linear summations, as it can negatively impact the perceived ability to generate a fatigue performance prediction or at least infer a prediction. It is with great peril that anyone should venture past the event horizons of applicability of linear elastic fatigue behavior.

There are numerous papers where outcomes have been accurately determined, even with multiple loadings crossing a horizon. In analyses that cross horizons, an accurate result can be predicted with clever adjustment of ambiguous factors. This may merely be "postdicting" an outcome. Postdiction is where calculations are adjusted with apparently minor mathematical factors, but these factors may significantly manipulate results.

One common technique for adjusting results is the application of a scaling ratio. One common ratio is (a/b-1). With this ratio, if b is varied between a and zero, the quotient can vary between zero and infinity. Therefore, any value can be obtained with outwardly small adjustments. There are calculations where these types of adjustments are fully justified, but always be wary and challenge these types of adjustments.

Always be wary of a test correction that required posttest adjustment, as it may only represent a curve fit to a known point solution. Only once a correlation factor is proven to be universally applicable within given bounds should it be applied more generally.

2.3 Curve Shapes

Stress-life cyclic-allowable data points are hard facts produced through testing. The data points represent the configuration tested in its raw form. These points are typically used to generate a design curve. The curve is presented as the material's fatigue stress versus cycles allowable. It must be noted that common curves presented are not pure material data. The curves are a product of interpretation of the raw data points with some level of shape expectation.

As with the common graphic depicted in figure 2.7, the same figure can appear very clearly to be two different items based on its surroundings and the observer's bias. Likewise, there can be a bias toward continued curve shapes. A researcher's bias may see shapes they are predisposition to expect.

A researcher may expect that the physics of fatigue are consistent throughout the cyclic loading spectrum. That is to say that a highly loaded specimen failing in relatively few cycles progressed to failure in the same manner as a lower-loaded specimen in many more cycles. This presumption has led to the very common implementation of constant curves when plotting applied stress versus cycles to failure.

What if the phenomena are not consistent? What if different drives dominate in different loading levels? It is most likely that damage method is affected by loading, which would make continuous curves less than ideal for design engineering analyses.

Figure 2.7 Seeing what you expect to see can bias judgment.

Curves constructed from data points need to best suit their intended purpose. As discussed, the intended purposes of new design and field support analyses can differ. It can be highly useful to have separate curves constructed using the same set of data points. Analyses can be more straightforward using different curves for product support versus product development.

Stress-life data is often fitted with a continuous curve for use in stress-life analysis (figure 2.8). It has become common to refer to the data fits as stress-life curves. It is very enticing to formulate a continuous curve through test data points. Continuous curves have been shown to accurately represent many physical phenomena in some instances. They can also be unprecise for other data groups.

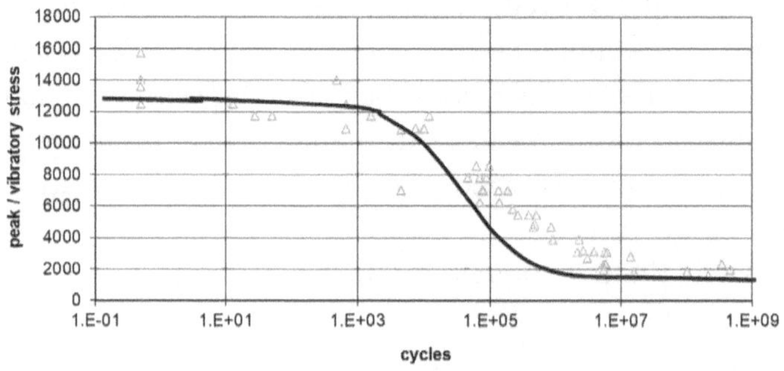

Figure 2.8 Continuous curve fit to data points.

It is proposed that in engineering, stress-life curve may represent multiple physical phenomena items having specific trigger points. Combining the phenomena into a smooth continuous curve may not be the most accurate representation of fatigue behavior due to mode changes. This leads to an engineering approximation methodology using piecewise linear representations being a more desirable representation over a continuous curve, like the one shown in figure 2.8. Piecewise linear curves are not new. Many existing works use piecewise linear curves. There is a representation dating at least as far back as Wohler. It is proposed that the piecewise linear curve, as shown in figure 2.9, is a method which is more beneficial in most engineering applications.

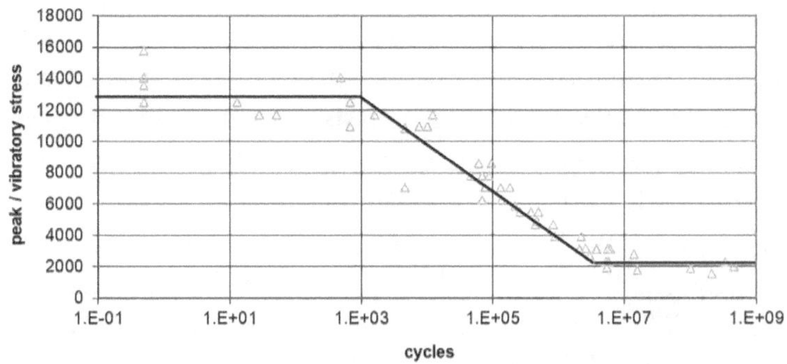

Figure 2.9 Piecewise linear fit to test data.

Piecewise linear fatigue curves present an opportunity to very clearly represent the trigger points or horizons where continuous curves can fog the transitions obscuring the limiting points. The ambiguity of the continuous curve makes them less desirable in engineer calculations.

Piecewise linear stress-life curves present very clearly defined horizons, both for high- and low-stress regions. An issue can be the limiting of the applicable stress-life curve regions where a Miner's rule type summation technique can be applied. Figure 2.10 shows a generic example of a continuous set of curves where the regions of plastic loading and unacceptable scatter near a singularity are removed from the usable region. Only a small central region of the family of curves truly fits the Miner's rule requirements.

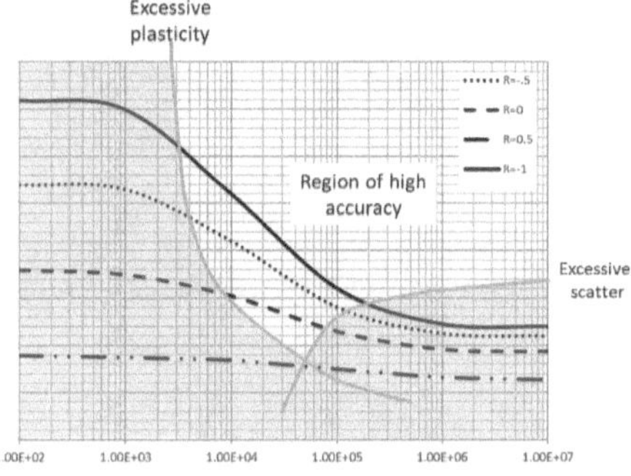

Figure 2.10 Linear damage summation limitation regions.

As can been seen in figure 2.10, the general concept of limiting applicable regions using continuous curves is easy qualitatively but challenging to quantitively. The use of piecewise linear curves more clearly delineates the regions in analysis. For an engineering-level calculation, the piecewise linear curves not only match the data very well: they clearly define the applicability region.

The piecewise linear sections are created using available test data, a straight line in semi-log space is used to connect the two boundaries. With stress and cycle data defined, two points are drawn in semi-log space. With the two points defined, three lines are used to define the stress-life cyclic behavior.

The first line is a horizontal line from one cycle to the upper excessive plasticity stress boundary point. The second line is a horizontal line from the lower-stress singularity cutoff where the primary damage mechanism effectively shuts down out toward infinity. The third line connects the two boundary points and represents the Miner's rule region of the curve.

Figure 2.11 shows how two data points clearly define the stress-life curve for the entire region of cyclic loading allowable stresses.

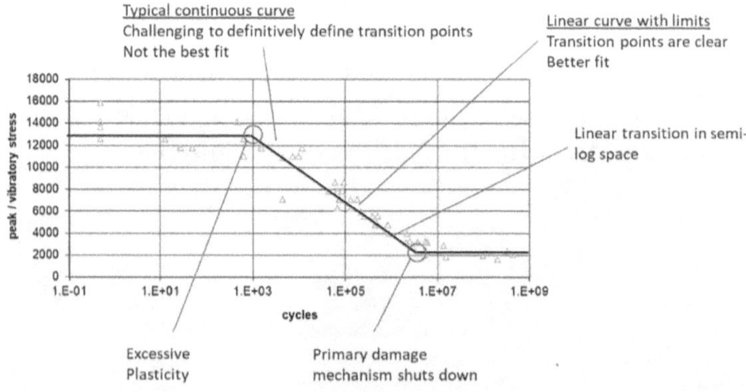

Figure 2.11 Piecewise linear stress-life curve.

2.4 Surfaces

The application of multiple types of stress-life curves has been discussed. Curves have been in standard use since the very beginning of stress-life methods. The question has to be asked: Are curves the most enlightening way to represent stress-life behavior? Or are they merely a remnant of an older methodology?

Whether continuous curves or piecewise linear curves, when it comes to loads, they are not exclusively a function of cyclic loading. Countless tests have shown fatigue performance to be a function of both steady and cyclic loading.

Being a function of two variables, fatigue performance produces a failure surface, not a curve. Historically, surfaces have been challenging to represent on paper. It can be difficult to select a value from a 3D-surface-depicted surface on the 2D page of a book. To remedy this, a series of constant life curves became very popular and useful in the representation of fatigue behavior in print. This procedure generates a series of curves, which are cuts through the surface, that are functions of both steady and vibratory loadings to formulate a typical constant life diagram (figure 2.12).

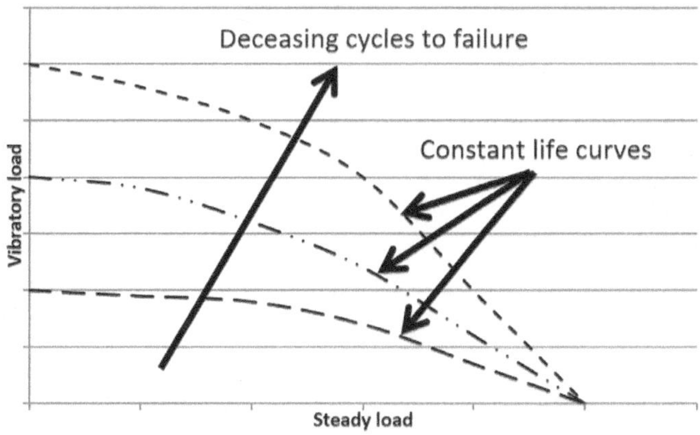

Figure 2.12 Constant life curves.

With current technology, picking values off a physical plot is rarely done. Using paper plots with discrete curves is an optimized methodology for past techniques but not for current automated techniques. Computer codes with fancy GUIs have become the norm. It is preferred to use the mathematical representation of the actual failure surface when using computer codes.

The inaccuracy of using a series of curves, figure 2.13, that depict cuts through a surface is only a relic of the past paper-based technique. It is more enlightening when a series of curves is expanded into a surface to represent the fatigue behavior. Plotting a surface of cycles to failure more clearly depicts the behavior of the material in its entirety.

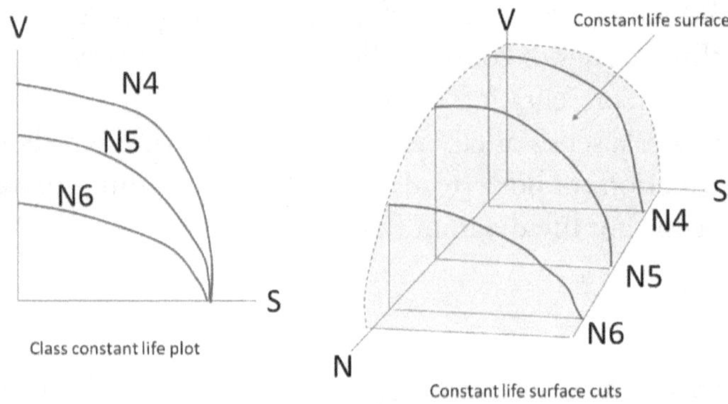

Figure 2.13 Constant life curves versus constant life surface.

Piecewise linear curves and surfaces add clarity and consistency to design curves. The curves present a simple method for constructing either piecewise curves or discrete surfaces to represent stress-life failure points for use in new product development.

The piecewise linear curves can also be used in generating a fatigue failure series of flat surfaces, as shown in figure 2.14, with two independent variables such as mean and vibratory, mean and R-ratio, and maximum and minimum stress to list a few. The faceted surface follows the same technique the piecewise linear did for the line. This type of constant life surface very clearly defines the limits of applicability of the fatigue analysis.

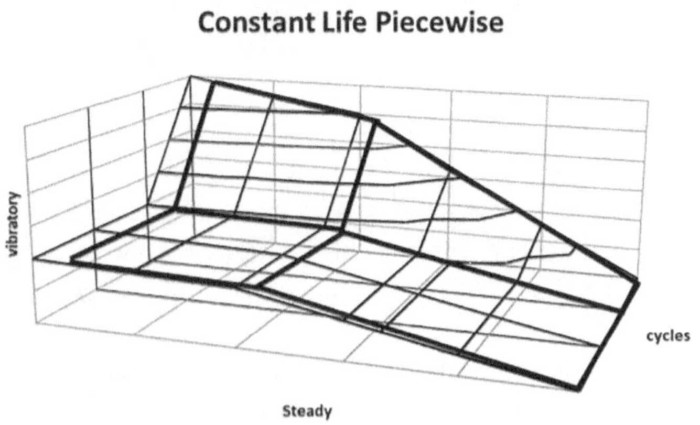

Constant Life Piecewise

Figure 2.14 Piecewise linear failure curves.

2.5 Type of Calculation

It is important to understand whether the task at hand is in product development where the analysis supports the creation of a component, which will not fail in fatigue, or in field support where the fatigue analysis assesses the fatigue failure of a component, which was designed to never fail in fatigue.

Product fatigue analyses needs to be divided into two primary categories. The two-category method can benefit analyses by using differing stress-life curve definitions. The two categories are based on new design or product support criteria.

Higher frequency loadings are addressed differently between the two categories for overall stability of the fatigue analyses. New product development needs to take a conservative path, while product support will often require a more median approach to field data.

Holistic analysis can apply loading rate knowledge to help separate cyclic region, be it cycle count or loading rate. As previously discussed, four basic load frequency types are proposed. The lowest cycle rate number of cycles is "on/off" rate cyclic fatigue (OCF), which can be thought of as an on/off cycling of a machine which can accumulate relatively few cycles. The next type of cycling rate is Low Cycle Fatigue (LCF), which could be a cycle per process or event. The OCF and LCF types of cycling have relatively few cycles and therefore generally are more consistently correlated with test and analysis.

The next two cycling types are considered high frequency and can contribute significant analysis scatter. They consist of High Frequency Fatigue (HCF) and can be envisioned as a gear-tooth frequency of a drive mechanism. And the highest cycle rate type, Very-High Cyclic Fatigue (VCF), may be a harmonic or other ultrahigh frequency loading.

An initial set of cyclic loading allowable curves is applied in new product development. In new product development, ambiguous regions of fatigue performance are conservatively addressed and designs revised on paper to improve fatigue behavior.

The second set of cyclic loading allowable curves are field support. Correlating with field experience of existing structures is a different and more challenging situation. When correlating field results, it may not be satisfactory to merely generate a conservative estimate of field experiences. For field support, a precise mathematical representation with highly precise correlation may be required.

2.5.1 New Product Curves

As discussed, there are two types of scatter in cyclic loading calculations. The first is within the physics of the situation. Being physics-driven, this cannot be avoided. It needs to be addressed as best as possible, and the level of scatter properly stated. The second source is within the calculation itself. This scatter can be caused by the mathematics of plasticity or working too close to a singularity. This scatter needs to be either eliminated or at least minimized. Addressing analysis scatter is essential in bringing the analysis process into control.

The first step in constructing new product stress-life fatigue curves or surfaces is to define the growth region or damage accumulation horizons. These are critical in establishing the loading region where linear elastic behavior without the issues of a singularity or plasticity can be applied. The upper stress boundary is where plasticity becomes significant so that history effects need to be tracked. The lower-stress cutout is where the singularity in the curve dominates. The growth region is a straight line in semi-log space (figure 2.11).

This piecewise curve simulation will most times fit data better than a continuous curve. Additionally, it very precisely defines the limits of the applicable analysis region. A continuous curve takes far too much subjective judgment to define limits.

These plasticity and singularity boundaries can considerably limit a cyclic loading analysis. Depending on geometric features, many metals will see a high-stress plasticity region encompassing cyclic failures from just a few cycles up to the 10^3 to 10^4 range. Many materials will see the singularity beginning to dominate around the 10^6 to 10^7 range. These boundaries will limit fatigue calculations to an analysis region of loadings, as seen in figure 2.15.

Using the holistic approach will aid in creating two separate yet supportive calculations to assess cyclic loading. Rather than combining all loadings into a single cumulative damage calculation, the knowledge of loading frequency is applied.

The first calculation addresses the high cycle loadings (HCF and VCF). These loadings with their very high rate of cycling and vast cycle count can be addressed as a quasi-static analysis using the lower singularity horizon as a static allowable.

The premise is that damage accumulates so rapidly as to mimic static failure. The calculation is a go/no-go assessment using the lower singularity horizon as an allowable. This calculation is applied to assure HCF and VCF loadings fall below the lower singular horizon.

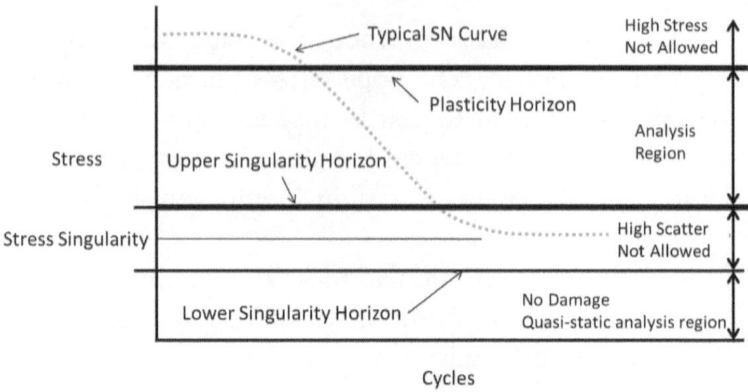

Figure 2.15 New product development curve regions.

The second calculation addresses the lower cycling rates (OCF and LCF). This is a classic stress-life calculation. The benefit of separating the HCF and VCF is that the endurance stress (singularity) is not required for a new product development cyclic-allowable curve.

Addressing the classic endurance limit or the singularity in new product development greatly aids analysis efforts by building on the piecewise linear curve technique. High-frequency loadings are held below the classic endurance limit and are addressed as a single static load case would be addressed.

Once the high cycle cases are reviewed and addressed with the go/no-go assessment, they are removed from the usage spectrum since, by design, they produce no engineering-level damage. The OCF and LCF loadings are now assessed using classic methods. To do this, the sloped portion of the fatigue failure line is extended from its endurance level down to intersect the zero-stress level (figure 2.16), which eliminates a singularity from the calculation. Not having a mathematical singularity stabilizes the calculation, greatly reducing scatter in predictions.

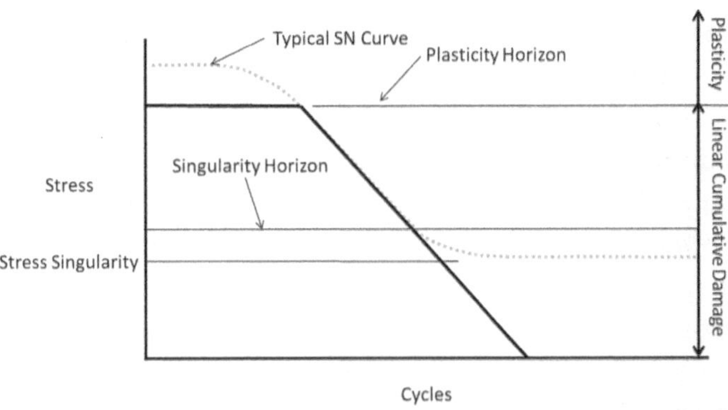

Figure 2.16 Piecewise linear data fit for new product.

Next, high stresses producing plasticity are assessed. The criterion for new product development will be no allowable repeated plastic yielding. The limit is shown in figure 2.16 as the horizonal line at the plasticity horizon.

One-time plastic events—such as shot peening, roller burnishing, or other plastic yielding—can be addressed by standard stress-life if no other or repeated yielding occurs. This criterion should not be limiting for the vast majority of design configurations, as repeat plasticity is seldom desirable in new designs.

The fatigue design curve has now progressed to having no plastic cycles and the lower-stress region having a continuous line from the plastic cutoff all the way down to zero stress. The elimination of the near-singular portion of the analysis greatly increases the consistency of the calculations.

Applying knowledge to divide the assessment into two calculations eliminates the extreme sensitivity of stress level to cyclic allowable in the near-singular region. This adds significant consistency and repeatability to the new product stress-life analysis process, bringing the method into better control.

2.5.2 Field Support Curves

Field support may not have the benefit of allowing extra conservatism, like is used in new product development. The standard criterion of field analyses is to precisely explain failures. Once a failure is explained through a collaborating analysis, the knowledge can be used to aid in correcting the issues.

Temptation is always present to adjust an accepted theory to help it in explaining a known result. This postdicting is not difficult. It can be very straightforward to tweak inputs until the desired result is produced. This begs the question: Was the prediction truly determined without prejudices to a desired outcome?

It is very possible that the applied theory was perfectly sound, yielding valuable results. It is also possible that inputs were adjusted in a prejudicial manner to show how well the theory works. Since corrective actions are usually based on the analysis, it is highly important to fully understand the inevitable adjustments and how they were determined.

When an improper theory is applied to resolve a field failure, there is a risk that the problem may not be completely resolved. It is also possible that the proposed solution is not the most efficient. And worse, a proposed repair can degrade the configuration if improperly applied.

It is possible that the field support analysis predicts stresses in the high scatter region of the classic stress-life curve (figure 2.17). This region is very unstable for predicting fatigue results. Stresses almost never can be determined to the necessary accuracy. Even with perfect stress calculations, testing results clearly demonstrate great variability in fatigue lives with nearly identical loadings and geometries. Care must be taken when there is a combination of uncertainty in stress values combined with test data scatter. Results need to be clearly understood and properly labeled if stresses fall in the near-singular region.

Like with new product, development loadings need to be divided into high- and low-loading frequencies. Applying knowledge will help with the analysis and its associated precision. Unlike in new product development, the analysis singularity cannot be easily eliminated.

High frequency loads (HCF and VCF) may fall into three regions: 1) flag for review, 2) high scatter, and 3) no damage, as illustrated in figure 2.17. Ideally, only nondamaging loadings will be found. Often, that will not be the case. If loadings are found above the upper singularity horizon, it is a red flag that needs special attention. If loadings are found between the upper and lower singularities, then significant scatter may enter the calculations. In these cases, a good-better-best conclusion may be all that is possible.

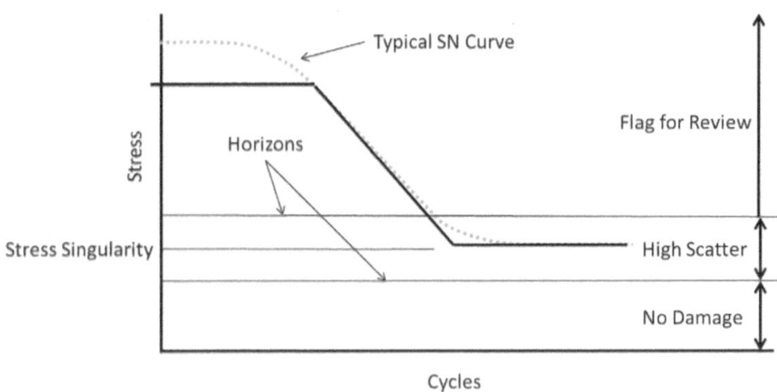

Figure 2.17 High-cycle field support.

For low-frequency loadings (OCF and LCF), the entire curve with its singularity needs to be applied. As with the high-frequency loadings, any findings between the singularity horizons need to be flagged. The inherent scatter accepted and identified. If stresses above the plastic limit are found, then strain life calculations or other plastic-cycling methodology needs to be employed. The linear cumulative damage region is where Miner's rule can be applied and produce highly controlled results. A schematic of the low-frequency loadings is illustrated in figure 2.18

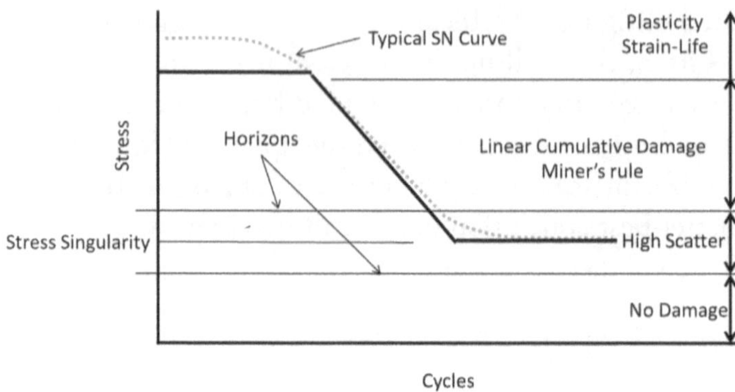

Figure 2.18 Low-cycle field support.

While it can be suggested that the low- and high-frequency curves for field support can be combined, it is beneficial to review high- and low-frequencies separately to emphasize the difference with loading frequencies.

2.5.3 Stress-Life Curve Summary

Currently, all fatigue theories require some level of adjustment. The amount of adjustment is what can corrupt the validity of a prediction. While it's true that all have built-in adjustments, some methodologies are better at hiding adjustments under quasi-physics-based labels, but all methods have them.

It is very important, especially in field correlation efforts, to examine all inputs. Every input has a significant impact on results. None should be overlooked or regarded as trivial. There is a requirement to control all adjustments to assure predictions are done blind. Otherwise, field predictions or correlations with actual results may have only agreed with post-dictions.

Analytic tools are invaluable in aiding with the investigation of field problems. Analytic tools can bring great insight toward understanding issues and with proposing solutions. They must, however, first prove to provide consistent accurate results with objective inputs. Analyses must clearly define any sensitivity to inputs and level of scatter of predictions based on the variability of criteria. Combining predictions with a level of confidence in those predictions will help in preventing future cost, loss of usage, and most importantly, injury.

2.6 Scatter-Needed Line and Surface

Identifying potential scatter in predictions due to loading, usage, and analysis must accompany the analytical results. Quantifying scatter is as important as quantifying predictions.

Even with precise finite element model stress solutions and accurate test data, there may be situations where (Huth) fatigue evaluation can be no more precise than good, better, and best. In these situations, only a general behavioral answer may be possible.

No developer wants to be in a situation where a clear answer cannot be determined. The reality of many situations is that generalities are all that can be determined. Further refinement only implies an accuracy that does not exist. It is important to quantify, as much as possible, the precision possible in any given fatigue analysis.

Scatter is commonly accounted for in reduced stress-life curves (figure 2.19). These curves may be referred to as working curves or design curves. The scatter-reduced curve accounts for scatter in the testing data.

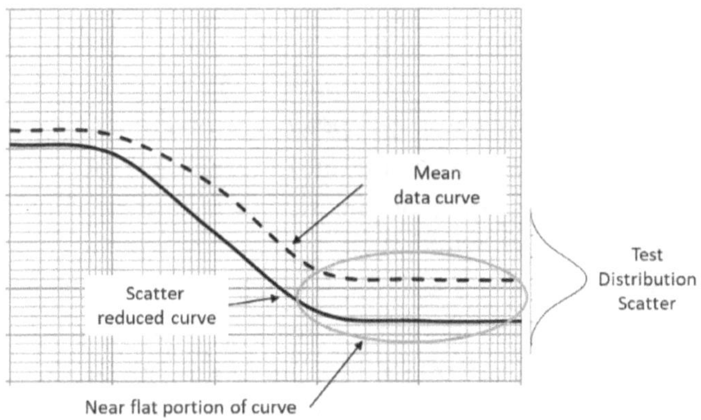

Figure 2.19 Work versus mean curves and associated scatter.

How is prediction analysis scatter using a working/design curve with a near-flat region accounted for? What happens for the loading levels around the near-flat portion of the curve? Could minute changes in predicted loads produce gigantic differences in predicted lives? This has been discussed as a by-product of working near a mathematically singularity.

How can a decision on how to respond to the concern be properly formulated? The ultimate result of the analysis is a choice on how to best address the cyclic loading situation. If the analysis is not accurate, it presents not only a technical but a managerial and possible safety dilemma.

A solution to this dilemma is to match an uncertainty value to the fatigue prediction. The uncertainty value allows stress-life curves and analyses to quantifiably account for uncertainty with fatigue predictions, thus quantifying the reality that there may all too often be no clearly definable value. Many times, the notion of a clear, single, definable solution must be abandoned. In reality, a single value that can be easily defended may not exist.

Reporting fatigue performance as a single precise value implies the value is highly accurate or that all predictions carry equal weight. Unfortunately, in many situations, nothing could be further from the truth.

It is highly beneficial to report a probability alone with any prediction. Just like it's typically done with polling—where accuracy is nearly universally given, for example—predictions may be stated as: outcome A has a 57 percent +/-3 percent probability. Adding a value similar to the +/-3 percent, or a range of fatigue predictions that net a given accuracy, is highly recommended in fatigue predictions.

Adding a scatter value quickly points the spotlight at the event horizons previously discussed. How much credibility would be given to that same polling prediction if it read 57 percent +/-40 percent? It would be considered worthless, like the fatigue prediction should be if it also contained unacceptable scatter.

The addition of scatter factors does not limit the application of fatigue theory; it enhances it. Properly labeling results will aid in making better decisions on the course of action needed to improve designs. It can improve technology development in helping to guide the way not just toward additional fatigue methods but to how to help reduce scatter in predictions.

The benefit of adding a scatter range to an analysis is illustrated with a simple example. In this analysis, a fatigue assessment is needed for a new machine which is designed to run at 25hz (1,500 rpm) for 500 hours. The machine will be cycled on/off every 6 minutes. The on/off cycling produces much higher stresses.

The cyclic stress at the critical cross section is +/-6000 psi +/-5% during on/off cycling. The running vibratory stress is 2,900 psi +/-3%. There are 50,000 cycles of on/off, and 45 million vibratory cycles.

At first the analysis uses a conventional cyclic continuous curve. From the allowable plot, figure 2.20, the range of allowable cycles for on/off is 325,000 cycles +/-25,000, or 325,000 +/-7.7%. The allowable cycles for the vibratory cycling are 10 million (far short of need) to 1 billion (a very high life margin), or a prediction scatter of 505,000,000 cycles +/-495,000,0000 (or 505,000,000 +/-98%).

No clear conclusion can be drawn as to whether the design is acceptable or not. User judgment and analysis scatter could greatly impact the final decision.

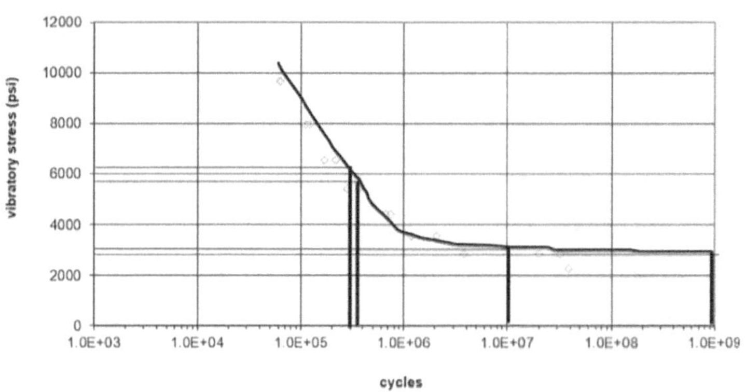

Figure 2.20 Analysis scatter with continuous representation.

Now, applying a holistic piecewise linear approach. The higher 6,000 psi prediction remains unchanged. With the high-cycle singularity removed, the predicted cycle count scatter is greatly reduced. Now the vibratory allowable cycles are 1.05 million to 1.1 million for the same 2,900 psi +/-3 percent, giving an allowable 1.07 million +/-250,000 (or 1.07 million +/-2.3%) giving a more controlled analysis scatter (figure 2.21).

The recommendation would be clear: the component requires a redesign. Of course, the high-cycle vibratory would have been removed from the Miner's rule under the rules for HCF and VCF. The conclusion and recommendation would be the same.

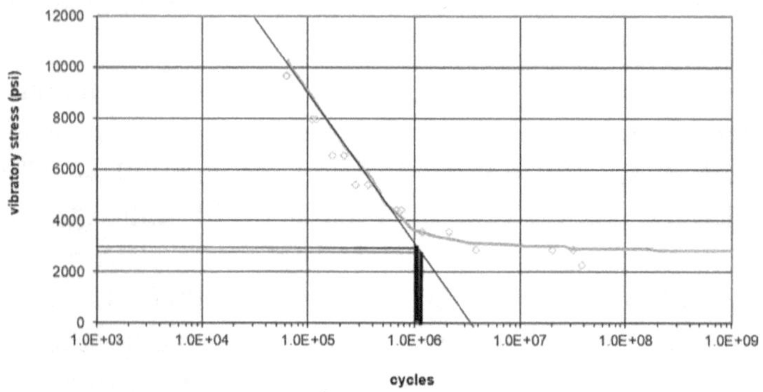

Figure 2.21 Analysis scatter with linear representation.

If this were a field assessment, the singularity could not be so easily avoided. For the field assessment, the forty-five million cycles are truly required. The stress level cannot be definitively declared a pass or fail. The conclusion will vary from analyst to analyst. Slight changes in how stress is determined combined with physical disparity at that loading level will combine to produce variation. A conclusion would only be that a field failure is within the realm of possibility. The conclusion would have to be identified as having high analysis scatter.

2.7 Conclusion

One key question to ask: Is your fatigue analysis in control? Like with any process, the first step is to be consistent and in control. A fatigue calculation process is, in many ways, no different than a manufacturing process. No manufacturing process would accept random results based on operator input or other factors. Why should fatigue analysis not also conform? If results are highly user dependent or have excessive variability in results, then fix the system before adjusting input factors on a case-by-case basis.

A holistic process is the only way to both have the necessary control while allowing required creativity. Holistic methods, by definition, bring all factors and knowledge to bear for an analysis. Addressing different loading frequencies (OCF, LCF, HCF, and VCF) is an important piece of information which should not be neglected. Using as much FEM information as possible is critical. Never oversimplify a current process to agree with an older technique. Always use every tool and all information to the utmost.

Engineers and metallurgists are two highly complementary professions, but in fatigue analysis, they can get too intertwined. Metallurgists look at fatigue for a microlevel where intergranular versus transgranular behavior is important. Metallurgists are highly involved with slip bands and the crystalline structure of metals. Engineers are more concerned with overall macro stress fields, geometric features of a design, and general fatigue behavior. These micro versus macro approaches to fatigue work very well together. The concern is when they are overly intertwined and physical phenomena are excessively extrapolated from one profession unto the other.

The conclusions drawn in this chapter are aimed primarily at the engineer's point of view. Stress-life behavior representation using continuum mechanics and macroscale features may not prove to be the most useful for metallurgist in developing new and improved alloys. They are extremely useful in assessing the behavior of designs using existing materials. Likewise, delving into intergranular scales with continuum mechanics-based calculations will not be highly productive for engineers.

New design and field experience correlation are two different fatigue topics. Different fatigue analysis approaches may be best to address the two situations. New design should use conservatism to net the highest level of probability and consistency for a successful design. Field correlation work must strive for the highest level of accuracy which may lead to a prediction which is overly sensitive to inputs and must be identified as such.

Critical limits or horizons of classical continuous mathematical classic stress-life curve representation can be challenging to decisively define. The nature of the continuous curve adds uncertainty in defining the limits of a theory. The curve may be a function of an engineering affinity for continuous curves and not the individual data points. They may not properly account for trigger points where damaging phenomena change rapidly. While a continuous curve may fit the data, it may not be the most advantageous engineering methodology for representing the data.

Piecewise linear representation of stress-life curves and stress-life surfaces can be highly useful in representing fatigue performance. The data points will many times be more accurately portrayed using piecewise linear curves. Not only is the data accurately captured in piecewise linear representation but transition points become very clear and objectively definable. Data transitions are clearly defined with associated limits in a piecewise linear fatigue curve, whether it is a linear line in a stress-life curve or a flat planar surface on a stress-life surface.

A statically based scatter value is highly useful in clarifying any fatigue prediction. Engineering calculations often support program and product management decisions, and the preciseness of their fatigue predictions provide valuable information toward the efficient management of any system. Including a measure of scatter is a critical component in a holistic approach to fatigue management.

Never disregarding information is a key constituent of holistic methods. Loading frequency is a source of insight that is too often neglected when all cycling is combined into a single damage value. Other factors—such as local stress field modeling, type of analysis, and required precision along with loading frequency—combine in forming a superior holistic fatigue approach. Inputting all relevant loading factors with a piecewise linear stress-life representation will identify when a fatigue life prediction is highly precise. It will also alert when predictions like good, better, best are all that are possible.

CHAPTER 3

Energy Methods

Practical Application of Energy

3.0 Energy-Life Methods

Force and stress have long been used in engineering to categorize fatigue behavior. Most likely due to familiarity and a straightforward analysis technique. What if stress is not a primary driver of fatigue?

Energy can be a more physics-based criterion for characterizing fatigue performance. The use of a total energy scalar could prove to be the primary indicator of internal damage due to cyclic loading.

Energy fits nicely with the second law of thermodynamics which states that entropy is increasing. Increasing entropy can explain cumulative cyclic loading damage.

3.1 Analysis Evolution

Assessment of cyclic loading is an important part of both design and product support processes. The assessment of cyclic loading impact goes back over a hundred years. It is rooted in the use of metals in load-bearing components.

Prior to metals, mostly stone and wood products were used to support large loads. Stone has poor tensile properties, leading to its use being limited to compression loads. The pure compression loading led to no concerns with cyclic tensile loads. Wood was used when regions of tensile loads were present. Fibrous wood produces are highly resistant to cyclic loading fatigue damage.

With the industrial revolution and its widespread introduction of metals with cyclic tensile loads, there quickly became issues with fatigue failures. Early on, the focus was with iron and steel alloys and their use in railroads and machinery. Later, with the advent of aviation, the research was expanded into nonferrous alloys, such as aluminum and titanium.

Significant progress in fatigue analysis has been achieved to date. Analytical techniques, test standards, and design standards have been developed to support the manufacturing methods of their day. Methods were optimized for the analytic capabilities of their period and used to support the manufacturing techniques in use at the time.

Many of the fatigue analysis methods developed, and still in use today, were created when pencil and paper were the only analytical tools available. Others were created for adding machines and slide rules. These analysis tools served product developers well. They helped create many iconic machines, but they are limited. Developers were constantly searching for simple techniques that would be useful to industry and product optimization. Handbooks, straightforward relationships, and simplified calculations were the norms.

3.1.1 Cyclic Damage Normalizing Factor

One simple technique is to directly relate an applied load (P) to fatigue performance, as seen in figure 3.1. While simple and straightforward, it can be highly impractical to use load other than for highly conforming configurations of a specific configuration. The issue with using loading as the guiding factor is the large body of test data required to cover all the possible design configurations. Loading as a fatigue criterion was proving to be untenable for industry.

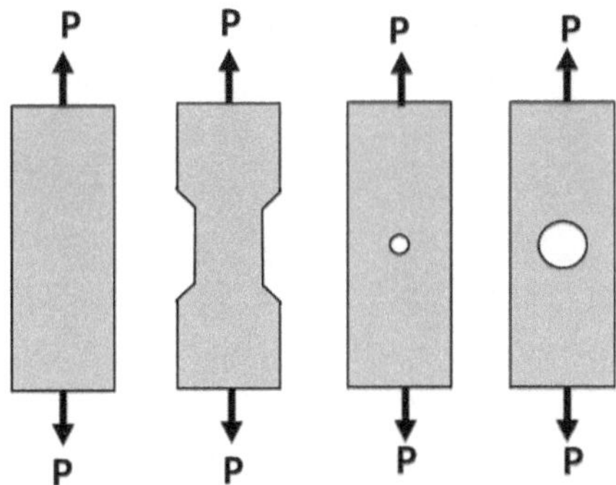

Figure 3.1 Applied load factor.

Limitations with load as a fatigue factor was remedied by applying stress. Stress proved to be a much more universal factor (figure 3.2). Stress allowed for significant reduction in testing scaling load by area. The ease of using load is made more universal by switching to stress. The downside to applying stress is the added complexity in calculating stress. Stress needs to be accurately understood in the local region of interest. The first question to answer is, What is the local area of interest?

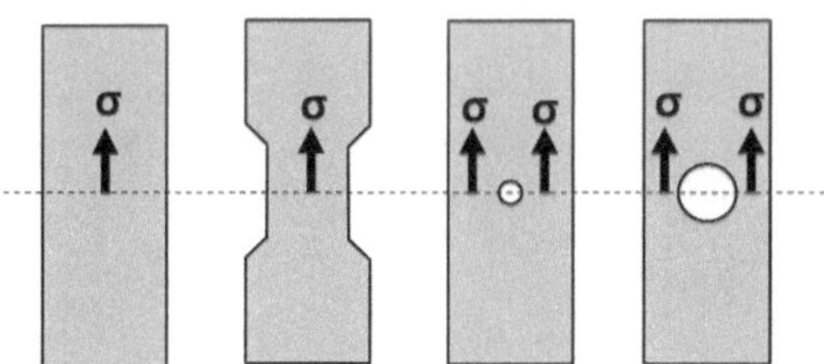

Figure 3.2 Stress factor.

Accurately modeling local stress before finite element methods was challenging. Determining gross section stress was fairly straightforward by applying general solid mechanics equations. The challenge is that fatigue requires knowledge not just for gross section stress but of highly localized stress fields. The theory of elasticity was commonly used for somewhat simple geometries and boundary conditions. These elasticity solutions generated standard textbook structural peaking factors.

3.1.2 Adjustment Factors

Stress peaking in simple round holes and other geometry features stress concentration factors was used to account for stress field variations near the geometric features. While simple geometric features could be addressed, the method cannot universally address many industrial development programs.

Early imperial evidence and intuitive thinking both point to a strong relationship between stress concentrations caused by geometric features and the level of stress applied to the component. The use of standardized stress concentrations offers a suitable methodology for product development. Figure 3.3 illustrates some simple stress concentrations and their impact on local stress fields.

Stress is a very familiar quantity to most engineers to normalize applied load based on area. Physical features like holes, chamfers, fillets, etc. were clearly visual at failure damage origin sites. Combining stress with a local geometry was a natural result. The method is commonly referred to as stress-life analysis.

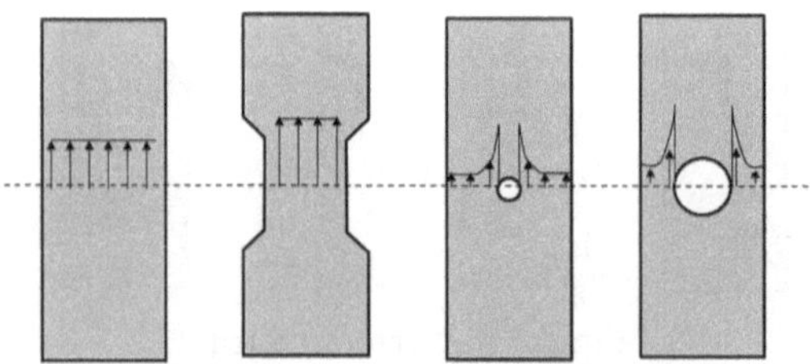

Figure 3.3 Stress concentration.

Stress-life fatigue analysis is still commonly used to assess the effects of cyclic loading on structures. The technique is typically associated with combining net section stress with a stress concentration factor. The methodology is employed based on empirically observed data that shows the greater the stress concentration, the lower the cycles to failure based on net section loading.

Issues arose when the stress concentration factor could not directly be used to assess fatigue lives. Analysis with vibratory and steady stress levels was found to require an adjustment to stress concentration factor (Kt) leading to a notch sensitivity factor (Kf) based on a material's sensitivity to stress gradients. Figure 3.4 illustrates how Kf is used to limit the peak stress.

A potential issue is that the Kf factor is an empirical fit with no generally accepted physical meaning. Kf is nothing more than a ratio of peak stress concentration stress to the level needed to match test data. It is typically varied based on stress level, making it a highly empirical factor. While stress concentration factors simplified peak static stress calculation, it pushed the fatigue issues into the Kf factor.

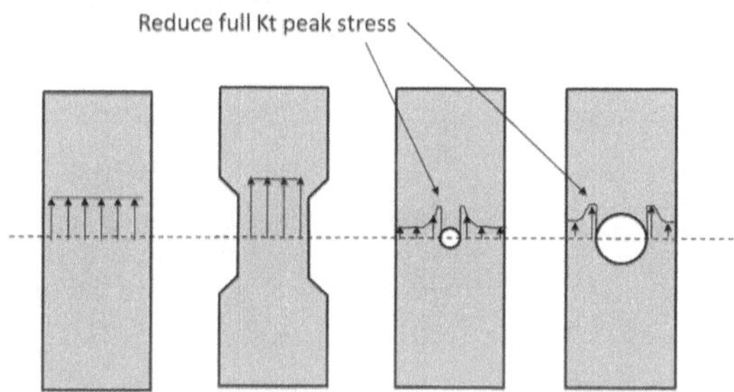

Figure 3.4 Stress gradient scale back.

Even when a clearly defined Kt based on simple loading and geometry exists, it needs to be adjusted based on a subjective empirical factor that is backed out of simplified testing. Kf is, at its core, an empirical ratio needed to match test data identified by a selected Kt.

It is also known that the size or amount of highly stressed material of the feature causing the stress concentration plays a role in fatigue performance, leading to an additional empirical factor for size adjustment factor. Stress concentration is a factor based on relative geometry, not absolute geometry. Fatigue is based on absolute geometry leading to the size effect adjustment to align test specimen size with design component size.

It is also noted that both factors can be highly subjective. There is a loss of elegance to the fatigue analysis based on observed features and normalized load when numerous imperial factors are introduced. While size effect is easy to depict as a qualitative concept, as seen in figure 3.5 where highly stressed regions are shown in cross-hatching, concerns arise when attempting to convert size effect into a quantitative factor for use in calculations.

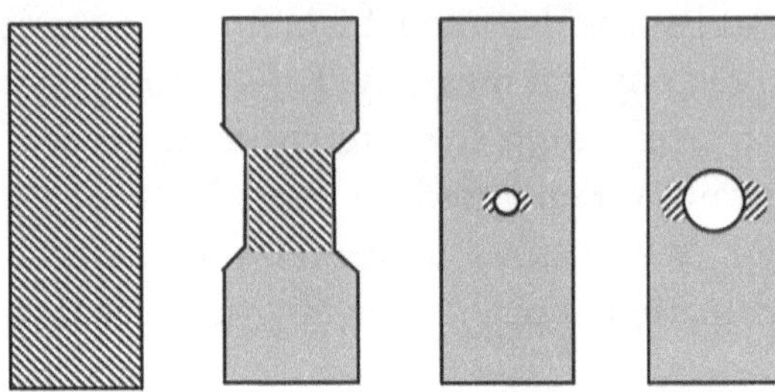

Figure 3.5 Size effect.

The use of net section stress, stress concentration factor, notch sensitivity factor, and size effect factor introduce significant user judgment into the classical stress-life fatigue analysis process using handbook solutions with simple stress calculations. The subjectivity becomes even larger when finite element methods are introduced. Using finite element methods with classical stress-life can produce a convoluted, imprecise fatigue analysis.

3.1.3 Complex Loadings

Stress-life analysis gets even more complicated when no clear stress concentration exists. What internal region should be used for net section stress for the example shown in figure 3.6?

Complex geometries and interactions between numerous features are simple to solve for with current computing capabilities, but they can make classic stress-life methods highly challenging. These challenges are often brushed under the rug in classical methods, producing what can appear to be more precise calculation than is actually possible. If complexed stress fields are reduced to simplified representations, then today's predictive precision is set back to when loads were calculated with pencil, paper, and handbook factors.

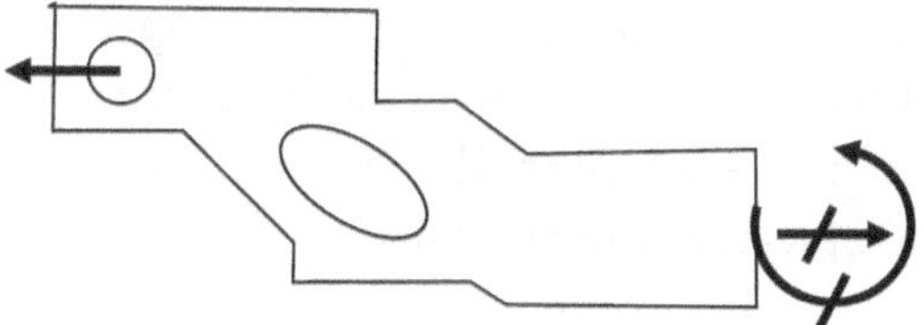

Figure 3.6 No clear nest section stress.

Current analyses often develop highly precise stress fields using finite element methods, as shown in figure 3.7. The highly accurate determination of internal loading presents an insight that was not available to the original stress-life developers.

Had finite element methods preceded stress-life development, they surely would have been more integrated into the calculations. The question today is, Why not better holistically integrate finite element capabilities rather than degrade them to fit a pencil and paper stress calculation?

There is information lost by simplifying a varying stress field to two numbers, such as peak and far field stress. A simpler, more straightforward technique without information loss is needed.

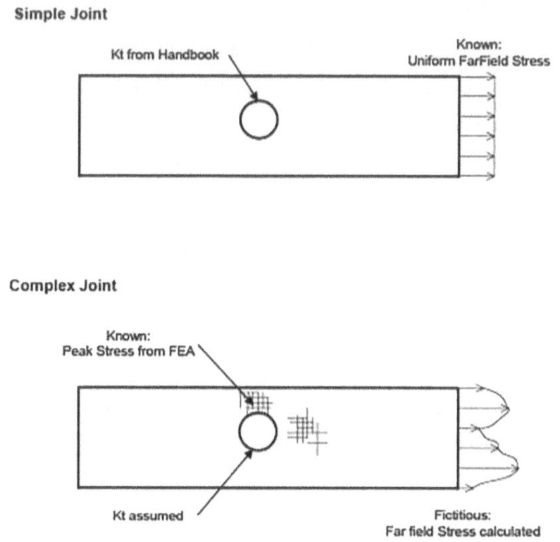

Figure 3.7 Finite element mesh example with variable finite element far field needing a fictitious stress representation.

Basic stress-life methodology was developed long before finite elements methods were made practical by current computing capabilities. Classic stress-life methodology was highly refined based on the technology of its day, but the early developers never accounted for the information fidelity finite element codes provide.

As outlined, stress-life was originally set up assuming a well-defined net section stress often obtained with classical analysis methods yielding a uniform net section stress. That stress was then adjusted based on stress concentration factors derived from either testing or elasticity analyses. Fitting theses inputs to test data of standardized shapes was straightforward, leading to a controlled technique.

3.1.4 Control

A basic standard for any process is that it needs to be in control. Calculations should be repeatable and reliable. If your process is so subjective as to be non-repeatable, it must be corrected and brought into control before any improvements can be addressed. Control is the core standard to any analysis. The more-physics based the process is, the more controllable and repeatable it will be.

The standard that carries through all fatigue analysis analyses is to apply all current fatigue methods to the greatest extent possible. These methods need to be as physics-based as possible. They need to apply all available knowledge and data. These philosophies are currently combined and referred to as a holistic approach and illustrated in figure 3.8.

Applying a holistic approach (Hoeppner, et.al.) is a well-founded principle. It was long practiced in unifying structural analysis technologies with stress-life fatigue calculations. This union was compromised with the introduction of finite element methods. In an attempt to quickly combine finite elements with stress-life, much of the holistic principles were lost by applying outdated stress analysis standards.

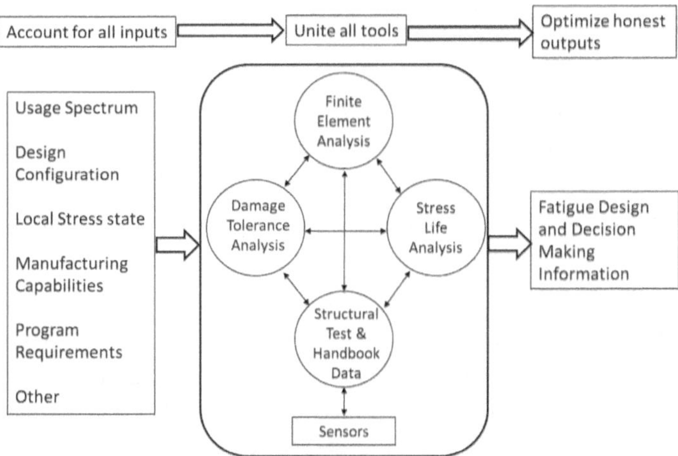

Figure 3.8 Holistic approach.

Much of the knowledge gained with finite element is often tossed away in an imprudent attempt to force it into a fatigue analysis that was optimized for pencil-and-paper calculations. This produces a very non-holistic fatigue system.

3.1.5 Fracture Mechanics

Fracture mechanics is an alternate methodology to stress-life, but the physics of the problem is universal for either. The only change is in how the physics are mathematically represented. Having said that, they both have their strong points and are highly useful when properly applied. They also both have weaknesses that need to be avoided to the highest degree possible. One possible area to help clarify their benefits is to better unify stress-life with fracture mechanics.

If done incorrectly, unifying stress-life with fracture mechanics can be even less holistic than either method individually. It's clear that a more physics-based holistic objective method is needed to bring stress-life with finite element inputs into control and to unify it with fracture mechanics (see chapter 4). These methods need to be usable by engineers to quickly and effectively generate efficient designs.

3.1.6 Expanding Horizons

Applying highly detailed finite element stress output can be challenging when attempting to employ classic stress-life. Figure 3.9 outlines how a decision to either include all finite element information or reduce to a simplified state can be hidden in a methodology.

The impacts of highly customizable geometry possible with current manufacturing technologies, such as 3D printing, add additional issues. Current manufacturing advances have made possible what was not even thinkable when stress-life methods were originally conceived. Finite elements give the ability to fully understand the internal stress fields of complex loadings and geometries. Stress-life needs to fully utilize finite elements to fully support manufacturing advances like 3D printing.

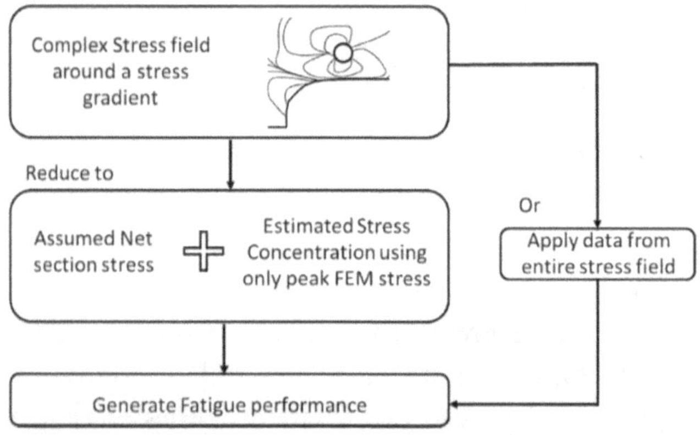

Figure 3.9 Combining inputs using finite element.

Currently, many methods for combining complex geometries, finite element codes, and test data require substantial subjective user inputs along with significant reductions in analysis fidelity. Adding subjectivity while simplifying data can hardly optimize a design. A new, revised version of stress-life better suited to work with finite element, unique geometric configurations, and fracture mechanics would be highly advantageous.

While stress is a continuous and familiar function, the fatigue damage caused by the stress field is not a continuous function. Fatigue damage has a single nucleation site. This point of origin is the only point where fatigue damage should be calculated. Figure 3.10 illustrates a few discrete initiation points where fatigue lives can be determined.

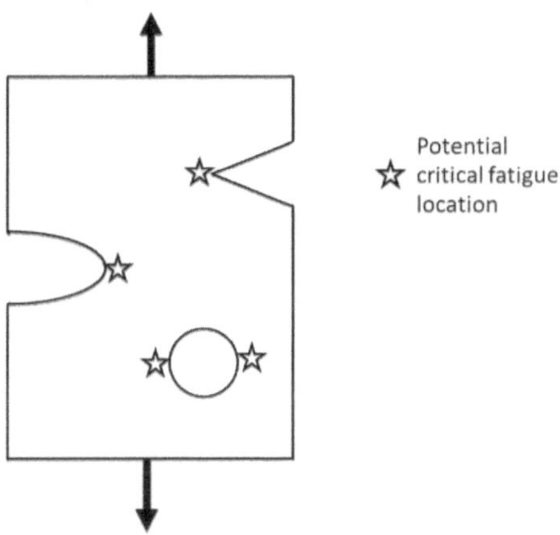

Figure 3.10 Potential nucleation points.

Fatigue lives are discreet scalar values that are defined at discrete locations. There may be numerous fatigue points on a single part, but the calculated damage is only valid at defined fatigue nucleation sites.

Energy in a given volume or surface is a discrete scalar, as is fatigue damage. Energy presents a more efficient and physics-based factor; stress may not be the best factor in determining fatigue damage. The application of stress tensors in determining fatigue damage at a nucleation point may unnecessarily increase complexity while also introducing additional subjectivity.

Energy is a much more physics-based driver for fatigue damage. Energy presents a factor which is based on work being done in a defined volume as shown in figure 3.11. Energy and entropy can assess any physical system. Using constantly increasing entropy and losses during energy conversion, the fatigue phenomena can be defined in highly physics-based function. Cyclic energy combined with a distance influence factor greatly simplifies fatigue life calculations.

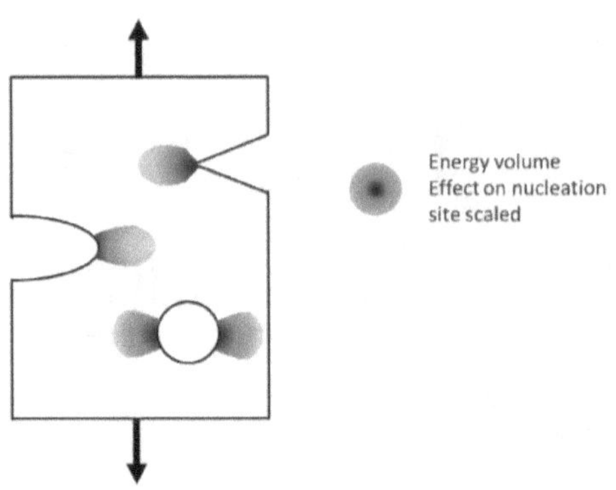

Figure 3.11 Energy nucleation volume sites.

Energy nearest the nucleation site will have the greatest impact on the micro damage that accumulates to generate fatigue cyclic damage. A material-based distance influence function can control the impact of a cyclic energy fields at a nucleation point. Energy in a zone rather than an often-fictitious uniform stress combined with an observed feature's approximate stress concentration factor will control fatigue damage.

The weighted energy in a zone will replace the subjective adjustments for Kf and size effect. For example, a very small hole will produce a small raised stress region, and in the lower limit, it will be inconsequential—meaning that the far field stress will be used, and the component will behave as a smooth detail.

At the upper extreme, a very large hole will have a significantly raised stress region. It will act as a smooth component, but it would use the peak stress. Figure 3.12 shows how a d-distance function varies this geometric proportion. This energy effect is highly similar to the stress scaling of Neuber and Peterson but without the need for a characteristic radius. Like with stress scaling, the size of a simple round hole's fatigue characters can be based on a loading somewhere between far field and peak.

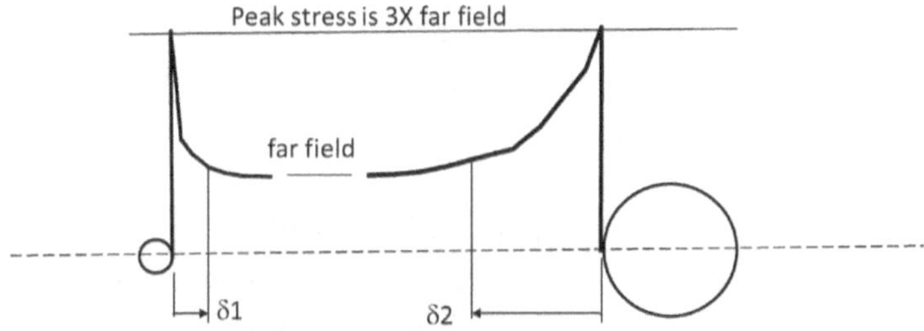

Figure 3.12 Volume factor.

3.2 Finite Element and Stress-Life

Currently, most complex structural analyses utilize finite elements. Finite elements can give much greater insight into internal stress fields than classic analysis techniques. Finite elements can very precisely define peak stress along with the entire local stress field. What it often does not clearly provide is a constant net section stress, which is the primary benefit of finite elements. This benefit is often seen as an issue in applying classic stress-life methods. This is a quandary in many stress-life fatigue analyses. To combine finite elements with classic stress-life methods, many techniques degrade all the detailed stress field information provided by finite elements into an approximated net section stress. How can it be a positive to degrade knowledge?

Often out of finite elements an approximated highly subjective net section stress needs to be associated with a classical stress concentration factor in order to unite the stress calculation with test data. In addition to the stress concentration assumption, a size factor for highly stressed material may be needed. Unfortunately, the region of high stress does not have a clear boundary. The side factor requires further assumptions and subjective inputs. Approximations, subjective judgments, and degradation of finite element data are all adding up to erode the precision of the analysis.

In order to utilize finite element results in classic stress-life fatigue analysis, it is common to 1) reduce all the stress field data to a uniform net section stress, 2) use this approximated net section stress to determine a fictitious stress concentration, and 3) combine theses values with an estimated high-stress region. All of this will forgo most of the benefits of finite element in an attempt to unite twenty-first century stress technology with nineteenth century fatigue techniques.

It seems foolish to diminish all the finite element stress field information currently available to fit a methodology, which was optimized based on precomputing analysis methods. Degrading finite element stress data fidelity into classical stress-life fatigue values requires significant judgment based on non-physics-based criteria. Not employing the capabilities of finite elements to the fullest while introducing subjective inputs can hardly be expected to be a holistic approach producing an optimized solution.

3.3 Selecting Test Data

Questions arise on how to best select material fatigue data for a design configuration that is created from testing of simplified coupons and normalized based on a stress concentration factor. In simple testing, a stress concentration will, most times, be clearly definable. The subjectivity arises in precisely matching the configuration to finite element results from a complex configuration. How is a stress concentration, which is defined as peak divided by net section stress, calculated using finite elements?

The net section stress, at least in analysis, is clearly defined and in control in paper/pencil/handbook stress analysis. Peak stress in classic methods is derived by multiplying net section stress by a stress concentration factor. This technique had a controllable yet imprecise determination of local stresses.

Finite elements can determine peak stress with much greater accuracy than classic hand analysis techniques, but that is only part of the equation needed in classic stress concentration values. So with finite elements, the peak stress is precisely defined, while in classic hand analysis, it is net section stress which is defined. This fundamental difference is the core of the issue in applying classic stress-life with finite element stress outputs. Finite element replaces the two scalars (net section stress and stress concentration) with a highly defined stress field.

Classical manufacturing and machining utilized may standard geometric configurations. Many of these finite numbers of geometries can be documented in handbook form. What happens when geometric shapes can be too numerous for handbooks? How will the additional configurations introduced with current manufacturing technologies, such as 3D-printed parts, be addressed? The complexity of 3D-printed shapes is often addressed by introducing highly conservative assumptions. Introducing assumed conservativism to address an analysis shortcoming will never be able to optimize a design, especially for the highly complex geometries made available with 3D-printed components.

It may be possible to simplify classical machining features that can easily be tested and standardized in tables and plots for use in stress-life analysis. 3D printing allows virtually limitless geometric shapes. 3D-printed shapes are easily handled by finite elements to define internal stress. The task is to assess limitless possible shapes without the need for limited test data of simplified geometries. A more universal standardization that stress concentration is required.

Stress-life calculations using classic methods present challenges in optimizing complex structures. Simplified stress-life analysis is not well-suited for simulating and optimizing many complicated 3D-printed shapes and stress fields. Stress-life methods, therefore, must be reassessed to be more physics based. Improved finite element integration with testing is mandatory to fully support current manufacturing and computing capabilities.

Uniting structural analysis with test data is one of the most critical steps in stress-life analysis, yet it can be nearly impossible to accomplish with simplifying assumptions added to finite element analysis of unique geometries. This leads to added subjectivity and loss of accuracy that can all too often be hidden in fancy software routines.

3.4 Energy Reduces Complication

The use of stress in fatigue life predictions complicates the analysis of highly three-dimensional shapes. Stress is a tensor which can become complex. This complexity is often addressed by use of values such as Von Mises stress, Max principle stress, or other simplified stress. This attempt to convert a finite element tensor into a one-dimensional scalar factor adds unnecessary subjectivity to the finite-element-based stress-life calculation.

Stress fields are now easily determined using finite element, and test data is precisely collected to characterize fatigue damage. The issue is uniting the two. That is where the subjectivity, hand-waving, personal preferences, and sometimes a little black magic come into play. Until the unification of finite element with test data is more physics based, the analysis will never fully control the stress-life analysis process.

Adapting fatigue analysis to fully utilize the power of finite element while reducing subjectivity and analysis complexity will serve to reduce cost while increasing accuracy. The use of a scalar damage value with more physics-based criteria along with finite element will advance stress-life techniques through improved stress-life finite element integration.

3.4.1 The Universal Scalar

Energy is a universal criterion which is a primary driving factor in many systems. It has been used as driver of cyclic loading damage in fracture mechanics. Energy is found in many applications from Einstein's $E=MC^2$ to how many calories are needed for a given mammal. It is proposed that fatigue damage accumulation is not a direct function of geometry and load but that geometry and load influence the primary damage driver, which is local strain energy.

Several energy equations include kinetic, potential, general, strain, surface, and caloric need energies. What they all have in common is that they relate a given volume of matter to energy. In all the equations, zero mass or volume results in zero energy.

- Kinetic energy: $KE = \frac{1}{2} M V^2$
- Potential energy: $PE = MHS$
- General energy: $E = M C^2$
- Strain energy: $SE = \frac{1}{2} \sigma\varepsilon$ (volume)
- Griffith energy: $E = 2\gamma_s aB + V *\sigma^2/(2*modulus) - B\pi a^2 * \sigma^2 /(2*modulus)$
- Kleiber energy: $E = M^{0.75}$

Not only is total energy within a volume the primary driver of cyclic loading damage but it is a scalar. Scalar values are much easier to deal with than tensors with greatly reduced mathematical complexity. Energy scalar values can be powerful fatigue damage indicators.

Applying physics-based scalars from both finite element data and test data can easily unite the two components with little to no subjectivity. The key to using energy is in determining how it is causing fatigue damage. How does the energy over a volume provide the driving force to initiate fatigue damage at a nucleation point?

Energy is clearly a universal factor in many systems. Strain energy can be used easier than stress-life predictions when using finite elements and other techniques. Converting from stress to energy will produce an energy-life fatigue analysis which can be easily integrated with finite elements. The application of energy to stress-life will also prove beneficial when unifying stress-life with fracture mechanics since they will both be based on local strain energy.

It is proposed that energy-life is the best standard for assessing fatigue behavior of complexed structures, especially when finite elements are utilized for stress field simulation. The use of energy precludes the use of tensor values and can be shown to produce much clearer physics-based rationale for associating simplified test article results with complex design configurations.

3.4.2 Neuber and Peterson Factors

It is well-established that applying the full Kt in fatigue analysis of ductile materials is overly conservative. A common way to address the issue is to apply a notch sensitivity factor. Two well-known adjustments addressing the notch sensitivity have been presented by Neuber and Peterson. Both use a distance-based adjustment factor. The primary difference being that Neuber uses the square root of distance. Figure 3.13 illustrates how, like with Kf, Neuber and Peterson reduce the peak stress when applying a stress factor in fatigue analysis.

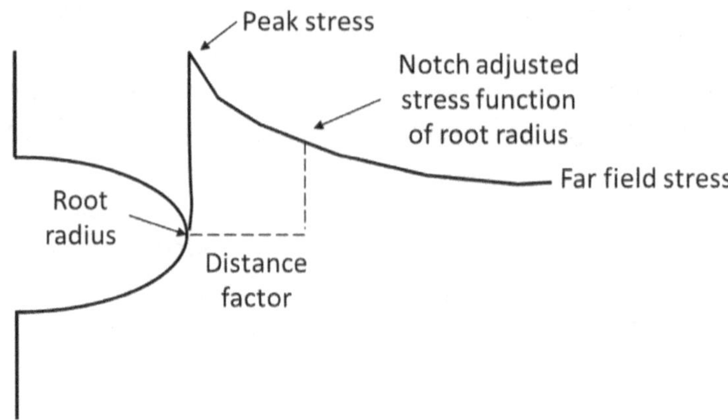

Figure 3.13 Distance factor.

Both Neuber and Peterson developed equations to convert Kt in Kf. They incorporate a characteristic material property to unite Kt and Kf. The characteristic material property is a test-derived factor that is based on material and local geometry. The user needs to determine the adjustment used to align test data with analysis.

By rearranging Neuber's and Peterson's equations, it can be seen that both methods apply an empirical factor to determine a stress value somewhere between peak stress at the surface and far-field at a distance away from the peak, as shown in figure 3.14. This appears to be an obvious technique to soften the impact of a full Kt. The issue is that the factor is highly empirical and only loosely physics based.

Where:

Kf = Notch sensitivity

Kt = Stress Concentration factor

ϱ & a = material property factor

r = Root radius

σ_{ff} = Far field stress

σ_{peak} = Peak stress

F(r) = scaling function

Neuber Peterson

$$K_f = 1 + \frac{K_t - 1}{1 + \sqrt{\frac{\rho}{r}}} \qquad\qquad K_f = 1 + \frac{K_t - 1}{1 + \frac{a}{r}}$$

$$\frac{\sigma_{fat}}{\sigma_{FF}} = \frac{\sigma_{FF}}{\sigma_{FF}} + \frac{\frac{\sigma_{peak}}{\sigma_{FF}} - \frac{\sigma_{FF}}{\sigma_{FF}}}{1 + \sqrt{\frac{\rho}{r}}} \qquad\qquad \frac{\sigma_{fat}}{\sigma_{FF}} = \frac{\sigma_{FF}}{\sigma_{FF}} + \frac{\frac{\sigma_{peak}}{\sigma_{FF}} - \frac{\sigma_{FF}}{\sigma_{FF}}}{1 + \frac{a}{r}}$$

$$\sigma_{fat} = \sigma_{FF} + \left(\frac{1}{1 + \frac{\sqrt{\rho}}{\sqrt{r}}}\right)(\sigma_{peak} - \sigma_{FF}) \qquad \sigma_{fat} = \sigma_{FF} + \left(\frac{1}{1 + \frac{a}{r}}\right)(\sigma_{peak} - \sigma_{FF})$$

$$F(r) = \left(\frac{1}{1 + \frac{\sqrt{\rho}}{\sqrt{r}}}\right) \qquad\qquad F(r) = \left(\frac{1}{1 + \frac{a}{r}}\right)$$

$$\sigma_{fat} = f(r) * \sigma_{peak} + (1 - f(r)) * \sigma_{FF} \qquad \sigma_{fat} = f(r) * \sigma_{peak} + (1 - f(r)) * \sigma_{FF}$$

Figure 3.14 Neuber and Peterson equations rearranged.

It's clear that the factor is an empirical method for selecting a value between peak and far-field stress in order to match test data. Neuber and Peterson both attempt to normalize the characteristic distance with a notch radius. For use with finite element, it is more straightforward to replace the characteristic root radius geometry with a material property scaling factor. Use of material scaling factors have been assessed by Garbo in his code FM and Urban et al.

Incorporating finite element strain energy with a distance adjustment calculation is an important step toward reducing sub-jectivity and user assumptions. The strain at a distance information presented by finite element offers additional knowledge on the state of loading. When using finite elements with a distance factor, the distance adjustment applies information from the entire stress field instead of the more limited stress at a peak point.

3.4.3 Distance-Scaling Factor

Energy cannot be created nor destroyed in a typical engineering scenario, yet perpetual motion is impossible due to energy losses and inefficiencies. This holds true for all physical systems, and the repeated stretching and contracting of materials is no exception. With each loading cycle, an input of energy may damage a stressed volume. This cyclic damage will accumulate until possible failure. Energy is therefore proposed as the key physics-based factor in determining failure.

Associating energy in a volume to its impact at a fatigue origin point is a key factor. Questions do arise. How do distance effects differ for different materials? As shown in figure 3.15, Does the distance effect along the surface differ from the distance into the material? These questions need be addressed in defining a material-based factor.

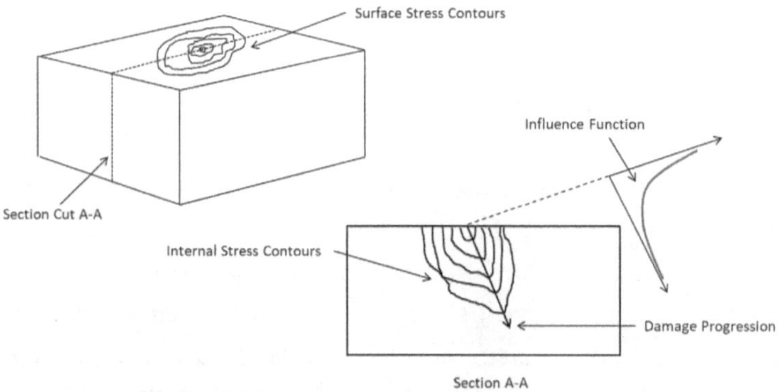

Figure 3.15 Surface versus interior scaling.

Plasticity will impact the distance factor. For many typical engineering metals with notched geometries, plasticity effects become nontrivial when fatigue failures are below 1e5 cycles. This is a very general statement which needs to be addressed on case-by-case bases. Any appreciable plasticity needs to be accounted for but is beyond the scope of this work.

Fatigue damage flows from high energy to low, just as water flows from high potential to low. This flow must be present to sustain fatigue damage. Stress-life fatigue damage is not a continuous function for an entire part. The damage can only be determined from a nucleation point. For uniform continuums, this point must be at peak energy density, with energy density decreasing in all directions from that point. A given part will have at least one, but may have many, fatigue point. These points may have differing fatigue characteristics leading to unique fatigue lives.

In testing of a uniform continuum, fatigue damage will always nucleate at a location where energy density declines in all directions. It will only be possible to experimentally determine fatigue lives for discrete points of a structure. Stress data correlation with testing should therefore only be done for damage initiation points.

3.4.4 Converting Stress Field to an Energy Scalar

What may be a highly complex stress-strain field can easily be converted to strain energy distribution and given a volume into a total strain energy scalar. How the effective volume is determined is a critical factor. The ability of the energy to contribute to damage at the nucleation site also needs to be assessed. If these factors are determined using highly subjective methods, then energy criterion will prove to have little benefit over stress-based analyses. The effective volume and distance determine the impact of the strain energy volume at the point of damage and need to be as physics-based as possible given an engineering environment. Care must be taken to assure objective criterion is used in determining distance factors.

In order to sum the impact of the strain energy field at the point of origin, it is proposed that the closer to the point of peak energy, the more impactful the energy will be on fatigue lives. As the distance from the peak increases, the impact the energy has will have diminishing importance. This energy impact distance is similar to the stress at a distance approach factor. Applying distance factors is highly similar to the work of Neuber and Peterson previously discussed, but in energy-life, it is a continuous function, not merely a point solution. The use of distance replaces the classic notch sensitivity factor allowing the energy field to replace the stress concentration and size effect factors.

Every cycle of peak to minimum stress will cycle the strain energy. Each cycle will not be 100 percent efficient, leaving some level of energy within the material. The energy will accumulate until sufficient energy is available to produce a measurable amount of material degradation. Initially, the degradation will take the form of slip bands, transgranular, and intergranular faults. Initially, there will be no clearly definable dominate crack. The damage will be more of a general nature within the material volume, as shown in figure 3.16.

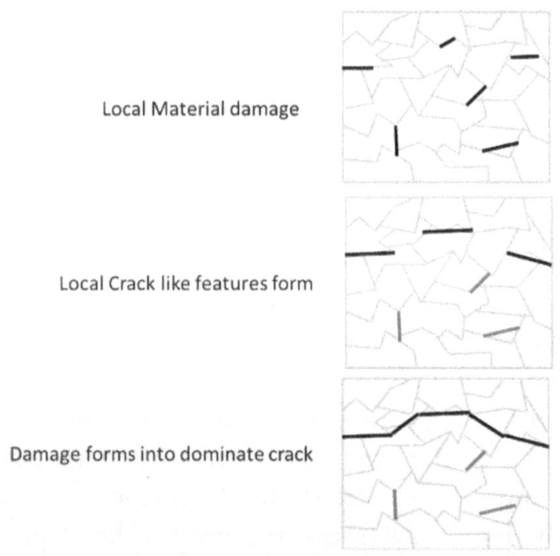

Figure 3.16 Growth progression of grain size damage.

A material distance sensitivity factor needs to quantify sensitivity to strain energy at a distance. Very brittle materials will have much different factors than ductile materials. Distance can either be along a surface or purely radial. If a distance factor is determined that is shown to be material dependent, it will be easily transferable from testing to finite element results. Energy at a surface may prove to be more detrimental than internal energy. If this is the case, then the influence of energy needs to be accounted for differently along a free edge.

In stress-life, multiple test configurations are used to represent specific geometries. They are often not easily unified into an objective factor. In energy-life, multiple test configurations can be combined to solve for material factors, making selecting test data based on Kt unnecessary. Testing of numerous geometries are combined into the material distance properties. With an energy density factor and energy distance influence factor, finite element modeling can clearly and precisely be paired with the appropriate testing data for a highly physics-based fatigue calculation. It will not be necessary to approximate Kt in selecting fatigue data. The fatigue performance will be a material property requiring no subjective selection.

Mean and vibratory loadings are used in stress-life calculations. In general, the two may have differing distance factors. It has been shown (Heywood) that a material's sensitivity to mean stress will be different than its sensitivity to vibratory stress. Commonly used constant life diagrams clearly show how increasing mean stress has varying impact on allowable vibratory stress levels. This holds for energy as it does with stress. Steady and vibratory inputs may require separate decay factors.

Applying a decay function to the influence of strain energy precludes the need to define a fixed volume. The function will naturally converge to a solution. All that is needed is a material distance decay property. This material property can be easily incorporated with finite element strain energy fields to allow for highly objective conversion of strain energy field scalar factors into fatigue calculations for each and every point-of-damage origin.

Applying a decay function to the entire stress field is a clear advancement from methods applying a single characteristic distance (Urban, 2010) (Neuber, Peterson). The techniques both address two critical characteristics. First is that stress-life fatigue life prediction is valid at a point of origin with stress decreasing in all directions from that point. Second is that the stress field data is used in selecting material fatigue data in lieu of a stress concentration factor.

A function H is proposed to represent the energy field from a nucleation point. The function sums the energy from the nucleation to a convergent location or the free edge of a detail. Additional consideration may be required if two free surfaces are so close as to significantly interact.

$$H = \int_{0}^{\infty} \left(\frac{EV_{x,y,z}}{F_v(m,d)} \right) \left(\frac{ES_{x,y,z}}{F_s(m,d)} \right) dv$$

Where:

EV and ES are strain energy fields over volume of material. Nonsingular field.

F_v and Fs are radial distance functions based on material (m) and distance (d) from the fatigue initiation point.

Distance cannot cross outside volume of a part and terminates at free surface.

F_v and Fs are experimentally derived functions

Summing the energy from steady and vibratory allows for independent decay functions. The separate treatment of steady and vibratory has long been shown to be important in determining the impact of cyclic loads. While steady stress, by its definition, is not cyclic and will not fit the energy per cycle analogy directly, it does influence the damage done by the cyclic loading and therefore is a proper multiplier of the cyclic stress. There is a large body of work that investigates cyclic and peak stress in a model of fatigue damage. Using a damage summation with vibratory and peak will work, as well as vibratory and steady, as vibratory and peak should also be primary factors in cyclic damage estimation.

3.4.5 2D Surface—3D Volume

In general, the 3D volume discussed will give a solution as to internal damage and associated fatigue performance. Using 3D volume provides a general level of fatigue cyclic capability. Using a defined point and the influence of strain energy around that point within a volume can determine the impact of cyclic loading on damage.

When a given fatigue cracking plane can be clearly defined, it should be employed as a refinement on 3D volumes. Additional knowledge on a primary damage plane will help in determining fatigue lives. Applying all knowledge in a holistic approach is critical in arriving at the best possible solution. A known 2D surface is clearly important information toward improved damage calculation accuracy.

A key factor in any endeavor is to always employ all available knowledge. Knowing the plane of fatigue failure is clearly highly relevant knowledge. In these cases, a 2D solution may be advantageous over the 3D method. The 2D situation may be highly similar to a planar crack in fracture mechanics.

3.5 Round Hole Example

A simple example using energy methods is presented for a 2D round hole in an infinite plate. The simple problem is used to illustrate the methodology. Keeping the geometry simple allows for a closed-form solution in lieu of a more complex loading, which would most often be determined using finite element methods.

The addition of a mean stress requires the use of the mean stress fitting function. The purpose of this example is to most straightforwardly present the technique. Therefore, a further simplification will make use of purely vibratory loading. Mean stress effects, if present, would have been accounted for in a similar manner.

3D loadings would be carried out similarly but with a more complex solution. It is left to the reader to explore and formulate the more complex solutions needed for a more general analysis. While a design and loading configuration may at first look to require a general 3D analysis, knowledge of a failure plane can often simplify the 3D configuration into a 2D planar solution.

This planar solution of a hole in a flat plate is selected due to its readily available stress field solution. The use of the stress function eliminates the need for complex finite element modeling. In a complex problem, finite element method with numerical integration would be an ideal solution.

Based on elasticity solutions, the far field stress is multiplied by three at the edge of the hole is true for any diameter given infinite plate size. The axial stress at the edge of the hole stress approaches twice the net section stress when hole diameter approaches specimen width.

For a very, very small diameter hole, the fatigue life approaches the unnotched life using the far-field stress. For a very large diameter hole in an even larger specimen, the life approaches an unnotched life using the peak stress. This is seen in the Neuber and Peterson factors. Both the factors rely on a material shape (radius of notch) factor and often require a size effect factor. Using a strain energy influence factor will be a much more physics-based solution. And its solution is based on a scalar.

The general form of the strain energy equation is shown in equation 1. The equation integrates the strain energy weighed by a distance function over a volume in 3D formulations or area for 2D formulations.

$$H = \int_0^\infty \left(\frac{EV_{x,y,z}}{Fv}\right)\left(\frac{ES_{x,y,z}}{Fs}\right) dv$$

Where:

H is the strain energy influence factor. It is based on the strain energy within a volume. It is defined by the strain energy factored by the radial distance from the predetermined nucleation point. R is the radial distance to the fatigue initiation point. Integration has no inherent distance limit. Distance cannot cross outside volume of a part and terminates at any free surface.

Vibratory strain energy (EV) and steady strain energy (ES) are strain energy fields over a volume of material. They represent a nonsingular field.

Fv is the distance influence function with experimentally derived factors for vibratory loading.

Fs is the distance influence function with experimentally derived factors for steady loading. While steady does not directly have a cyclic energy, it does influence the cyclic portion of the damage function.

Using energy to assess fatigue damage can be as complex or simple as needed. The level of complexity is determined by the user but should always be kept to the lowest level necessary. Simple elegant expressions will most often best represent the physical reality.

In this example, a simple exponential decay function is applied. This simple function can work very well for a basic application. Custom decay functions may be more precise for specific materials and configurations.

The first step is to simplify the energy solution to eliminate terms associated with steady stress, as shown in equation 2.

$$H = \int_0^\infty \left(\frac{EV_{x,y,z}}{e^{\alpha R}} \right) dv$$

The second step is to reduce the solution to a 2D equation, as shown in equation 3. In this example, the loading does not vary through the thickness; therefore, the solution makes use of that knowledge.

$$H = \int_0^\infty \left(\frac{EV_{x,y}}{e^{\alpha R}} \right) da$$

The addition of the stress field data into the equation further advances the solution. The known solution for uniaxial tension around a round hole in an infinite plate, as shown in figure 3.17, is presented in both polar and rectangular coordinate systems (see equations 4 to 9). In the classic solution, r is the distance from the center of the hole. In the strain energy methodology, it is the distance from the peak stress that is required. The value r is transformed to R, with R being the distance from the peak stress.

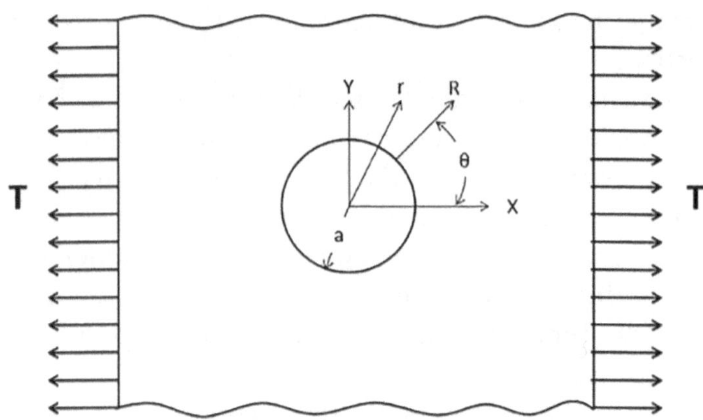

Figure 3.17 Tension with a circular hole.

After applying the boundary conditions and solving the elasticity problem, the stress field for general loading in the body is found.

$$\sigma_r = \frac{T}{2}\left(1 - \frac{a^2}{r^2}\right) + \frac{T\cos(2\theta)}{2}\left(\frac{3a^4}{r^4} - \frac{4a^2}{r^2} + 1\right)$$

$$\sigma_\theta = \frac{T}{2}\left(1 + \frac{a^2}{r^2}\right) - \frac{T\cos(2\theta)}{2}\left(\frac{3a^4}{r^4} + 1\right)$$

$$\sigma_{r\theta} = \frac{T\sin(2\theta)}{2}\left(\frac{3a^4}{r^4} - \frac{4a^2}{r^2} - 1\right)$$

in cartesian coordinates

$$\sigma_x(r,\theta) = T - T\frac{a^2}{r^2}\left(\frac{3}{2}cos2\theta + cos4\theta\right) + T\frac{3a^4}{2r^4}cos4\theta$$

$$\sigma_y(r,\theta) = -T\frac{a^2}{r^2}\left(\frac{1}{2}cos2\theta - cos4\theta\right) + T\frac{3a^4}{2r^4}cos4\theta$$

$$\tau_{xy}(r,\theta) = -T\frac{a^2}{r^2}\left(\frac{1}{2}sin2\theta - sin4\theta\right) + T\frac{3a^4}{2r^4}sin4\theta$$

The stress solution is further simplied by applying additional knowledge of the loading. In this classic solution, it can be deduced that the fatigue damage will nucleate at one of two locations. The locations are at 90- and 270-degree clocking positions with respect to the loading direction. It can be further seen that the damage will progress in a straight line following the peak stress. The line of progressing damage will follow radially outward from either or both of the 90 and 270 locations.

Since the two locations are equivalent, only one will be reviewed. The stress fields are now simplified by setting theta equal to a constant ninety degrees.

In the strain energy methodology, it is the distance from the peak stress that is required. The value r is transformed to R in equation 10, with R being the distance from the peak stress.

$$r = R + a$$

The stress solution is now simplified to the axial load at the 90-degree cracking location in equations 11 and 12:

$$\sigma(r) = T\left[1 + \frac{a^2}{2r^2} + \frac{3a^4}{2r^4}\right]$$

$$\sigma(R) = T\left[1 + \frac{a^2}{2(R+a)^2} + \frac{3a^4}{2(R+a)^4}\right]$$

T = far field tension stress.
a = hole radius.
r = radial distance from hole center.
R = radial distance from the peak stress.
The stress function is integrated over a volume to obtain the total strain energy. The energy equation contains not only stress values but also modulus of elasticity. Again, applying knowledge that the configuration uses elastic isotropic materials with uniform properties allows for moving the modulus term out of the integration, as shown in equation 13.

$$U = \int \frac{\sigma^2}{2E} dv = \frac{1}{2E} \int \sigma^2 dv$$

Substituting the stress function into the energy equation nets the total strain energy. The strain energy is presented as a function of radial distance from the peak stress at the surface of the hole. Note that this is a simplified solution with unit thickness. Stress is uniform through thickness. Cyclic loading damage follows a known line progressing radially outward from a known nucleation point. The energy damage accumulation factor is determined for this formulation.

$$U = \frac{T^2}{2E} \int \left(1 + \frac{a^2}{2(R+a)^2} + \frac{3a^4}{2(R+a)^4}\right)^2 dR$$

$$U = \frac{T^2}{2E} \int \left(1 + \frac{a^2}{(R+a)^2} + \frac{13a^4}{4(R+a)^4} + \frac{3a^6}{2(R+a)^6} + \frac{9a^8}{4(R+a)^8}\right) dR$$

Equations 14 and 15 above represents the strain energy of the failure surface area. The included area for this simplified stress field is infinite, so the strain energy would also be infinite. Once again, by applying knowledge, the solution can be modified to better reflect the physics. The foundation of the energy method is that damage is a function of local energy. Local energy implies that as distance from peak energy density (nucleation point) increases, its influence on local damage decreases.

To account for distance from the nucleation point (peak energy density point), a distance influence factor is added to the strain energy field. The distance influence factor is a material property. It can vary greatly based on numerous factors. A simple straightforward exponential function is used in this example to show how even simple formulations can be useful. In equation 16, the influence factor is introduced into the strain energy equation to create the strain energy damage function.

$$H = \frac{T^2}{2E} \int_a^\infty \left(\frac{1 + \dfrac{a^2}{(R+a)^2} + \dfrac{13a^4}{4(R+a)^4} + \dfrac{3a^6}{2(R+a)^6} + \dfrac{9a^8}{4(R+a)^8}}{e^{\alpha R}} \right) dR$$

To solve for the influence function weight factor (alpha), the stress field for the plate with a round hole is compared to the energy field of a smooth or uniformly stressed configuration. This is similar to the stress-life method where a smooth Kt=1 curve is used as the baseline for fatigue life calculations.

For a constant stress field (Kt=1.0), the stress will be uniform throughout the part. To adjust the strain energy function from the notched (hole) configuration to a smooth (unnotched) configuration, a factor is required on the far-field stress multiplier T. The ratio is represented as B. H_c represents the strain energy factor for the smooth constant stress configuration shown in equation 17.

$$H_c = \frac{B^2 T^2}{2E} \int_a^\infty \left(\frac{1}{e^{\alpha R}} \right) dR$$

It is hypothesized that local energy controls local damage accumulation, and damage accumulation controls fatigue degradation. This is based on the premise that converting applied work to internal energy is never 100 percent efficient so that there will be a buildup of damage that may eventually coalesce into a fatigue crack. If alpha is shown to be a material property, then it should collapse all notched and smooth data for a given material onto a single plot. Therefore, the fatigue data for the plate with a hole is equivalenced with the smooth unnotched configuration (shown in equation 18).

Set H= Hc

Like in stress-life fatigue life curves (chapter 2), energy fatigue life curves may be constructed using two limits and a straight line in semi-log space. For most, if not all, structural metals, the limits are 1) significant plastic yielding at the high loading limit and 2) endurance, or no significant local damage at the low end of the loading limit. The two limits are connected with a straight line in semi-log space (see figure 3.18).

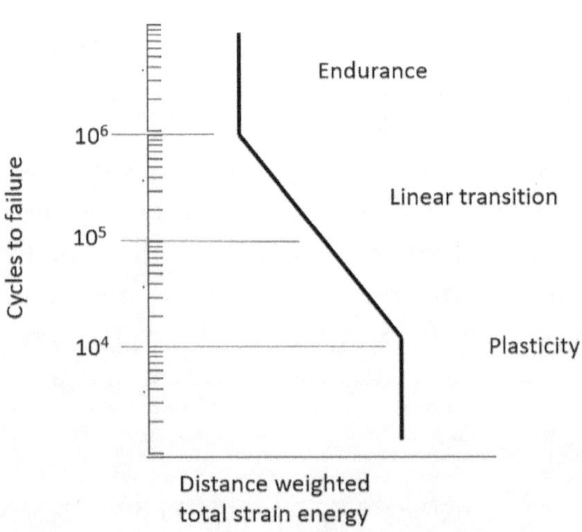

Figure 3.18 Typical energy-life plot.

This example is presented using a typical set of values for aerospace aluminum. In traditional stress-life curves, the upper loading limit is at a stress value which nets approximately 10e4 cycles to failure. The lower loading limit is a loading netting 10e6 cycles to failure. These values are adjustable based on many factors. Once determined, they should be supported by test data.

The distance influence factor is solved for using the upper- and lower-stress levels. In the solution, a further complication may arise when two values require a single loading factor to collapse the data to a single line which converges at both 10e4 and 10e6 limits. Collapsing two points based on fitting a single factor may require some level of adjustment to optimize the solution.

Some experimental data has shown that the lower and upper loading levels cannot precisely be collapsed to unifying points using a single distance influence factor which is based purely on material. This can be due to scatter in data.

Typical curve fits may require a variable which is adjusted using loadings. The loading factor can be evident based on stress-life curves based on experimental results. The factor may not be required to stay within engineering required precision.

Factors based on loading can easily be introduced, but in many engineering-level calculations, the data can be curve fit so that a loading factor complication is not required. Remember that the goal of engineering is successful designs, not closed-form solutions.

Any fatigue life prediction using current methods does require a level of subjective inputs. This is still true for energy-life. Therefore, only if it is truly required should a loading factor be added. It is strongly preferred to not use a loading factor. In this example, the data fit will be adjusted to net a pure material-based factor. In many design cases, this will be possible while constructing conservative design curves.

It is noted that this example requires a rational limit to the size of the geometric features. It is fully possible that the equation may solve for geometries in the extreme of size, shape, and complexity, but one needs to be reminded that calculations are merely extensions of experimental data. That test data may not apply in the extreme being assessed, so neither will the equation. If geometry is in the extreme, then additional experimental data will be needed.

Now solving this example for alpha by deriving a single distance influence factor using loading data at two constant N cycles (N=10e4 and N=10e6). To collapse the stress life into a single energy-life line in semi-log space.

It is noted that the test data is generated using a finite-sized specimen. The simplified solution is for an infinite body. Finite elements would have easily accounted for the geometry. Since the objective of this example is to demonstrate the overall method, the test data is applied directly to the infinite body solution.

The example is for an infinite-sized volume with a given hole diameter. Therefore, the integration has an infinite upper limit. This is not a concern since the energy influencing the point of nucleation will converge. This is a significant point. No user input would be required. No assumption is required on applicable stress zones or stress concentration factors. Once a material distance factor is derived, it will converge over a given distance.

There will be cases where the detail geometry is so small that the distance factor has not converged before reacting a physical limit. In this case, the distance is too small to separate the influence of multiple features, then an expanded solution is required.

Generic aerospace grade aluminum data at R=-1 (no steady stress) is used for this example. Two points are derived from test data at both 10e4 and 10e6 cycles to failure. The stress value for the notched configuration at 10e6 is adjusted to allow for a purely alpha-based influence factor solution. The raw test-based factors are listed below:

Smooth (Kt=1) 52 ksi vibratory at N=1e4

Smooth (Kt=1) 24 ksi vibratory at N=1e6

Notched (Kt=3) 20 ksi vibratory at N=1e4

Notched (Kt =3) 10 ksi vibratory at N=1e6

The objective is to show that the multiple stress-based curves based on geometric features can be collapsed into a single local energy-based criterion, as shown in figure 3.19.

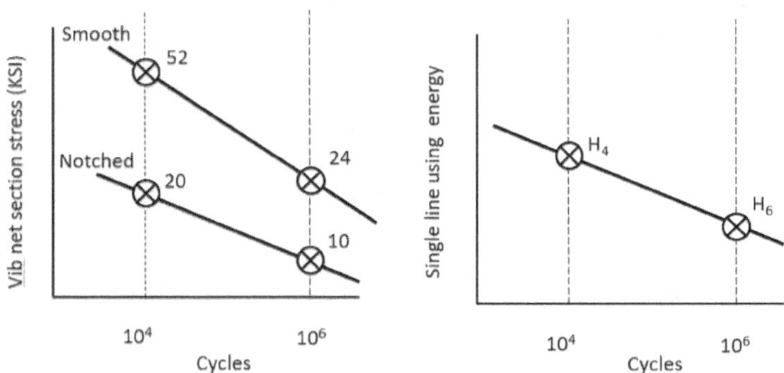

Figure 3.19 Stress-based versus energy-based curve comparisons.

The equation to solve for alpha is seen in equation 19. With "adjustable" notched data at N=1e6, only one equation is required, and it can be set up at any location within the bounds of the data. The example utilizes the 1e4 data.

$$\frac{B^2 T^2}{2E} \int_a^\infty \left(\frac{1}{e^{\alpha R}}\right) dr$$

$$= \frac{T^2}{2E} \int_a^\infty \left(\frac{1 + \dfrac{a^2}{(R+a)^2} + \dfrac{13a^4}{4(R+a)^4} + \dfrac{3a^6}{2(R+a)^6} + \dfrac{9a^8}{4(R+a)^8}}{e^{\alpha R}}\right) dR$$

At N = 1e4 → B = 52/24 = 2.1667.

At N = 1e6 → B = 20/9.231 = 2.1667 Adjusted 10 ksi 1e6 lower stress value to match B. This is a pseudo stress factor.

At N = 1e4.

$$B^2 \int_a^\infty \left(\frac{1}{e^{\alpha R}}\right) dr$$

$$= \int_a^\infty \left(\frac{1 + \dfrac{a^2}{(R+a)^2} + \dfrac{13a^4}{4(R+a)^4} + \dfrac{3a^6}{2(R+a)^6} + \dfrac{9a^8}{4(R+a)^8}}{e^{\alpha R}}\right) dR$$

The energy solution is based on test data. In a notched versus smooth test data comparison, the data will exhibit a trend. As notch size trends toward zero, the notched configuration tends toward the smooth specimen results at its far-field loading. As the notch trends toward infinite, the data trends toward smooth data at the peak or edge of the notch. The test data used in this example was generated using specimens having a one-fourth diameter round hole. Therefore, the radius a equals 0.125 inch in this solution shown in equation 21.

At N = 1e4.

$$2.167 \int_{0}^{\infty} \left(\frac{1}{e^{\alpha R}} \right) dR$$

$$= \int_{0}^{\infty} \left(\frac{1 + \dfrac{.0625}{(R+.125)^2} + \dfrac{.0127}{(R+.125)^4} + \dfrac{.000366}{(R+.125)^6}}{e^{\alpha R}} \right) dR$$

Solving for alpha nets a value of 97.84. This solution is valid for any loading or geometry given the constraints of the test data. Currently, fatigue life predictions are all based on test data. Test data should never be excessively extrapolated. These limits apply to any fatigue technology, including energy-life.

The calculated distance impact factor provides a very good engineering-level adjustment to the data curve. Since two equations are being fit (low-stress endurance and high-stress plasticity) are being fit to make a more precise engineering fit, the endurance stress of the notched geometry may need to be adjusted to improve data correlation for the piecewise linear fit.

This example can be expanded to cover many design configurations. The added complexity of loadings and geometries can be easily solved using finite element codes. Finite element codes can quickly and easily calculate strain energy densities. The next step is to merely apply the strain energy density distance influence factor to determine the total strain energy at the nucleation site. Artificial values like stress concentration, net section stress, and characteristic distance are no longer required.

By combining existing test data, the SEDF (strain energy distance factor) can be determined for a material of interest. The full strain energy data available with finite elements is applied to determining a scalar value which drives the cyclic loading damage at a nucleation zone.

3.6 Conclusion

Classic stress-life has proven to be a highly useful tool. Finite elements have also proven to be a highly useful tool. Testing is invaluable in engineering calculations. Excessive judgment has too often been used in attempts to unite these three technologies in a very non-holistic manner.

Trying to force current finite element output into a stress-life technique which was developed, refined, and accepted for slide rule techniques cannot optimize results. A technique is required which can fully utilize the power of finite element in fatigue without introducing excessive subjective inputs. Highly precise finite element results give great insight into local stress fields. Finite elements should never have its capabilities reduced to fit outdated stress-life input requirements resulting in significant loss of knowledge.

All too often highly precise finite element stress field output is reduced to a user subjective determination of a pseudo net section stress which is then combined with a finite element peak stress to calculate a pseudo stress concentration. The user defined net section stress is combined with the subjective stress concentration to subjectively select what test data to employ.

Once the stress concentration is determined, it may require a subjective size factor adjustment. The test data is then compared with the subjective net section stress to determine fatigue damage. This process may work for simple geometries and loadings but will never be capable of optimizing highly complex configurations. This technique often results in excessive curve-fitting factors and testing.

Optimized fatigue analysis is required to develop highly effective structures. While currently there remains some level of subjectivity in all fatigue calculations, the more objective a procedure, the more controlled and precise the outcome. A more physics-based union of finite element and test data will greatly help in developing holistic designs. The nearly infinite geometric possibilities of 3D-printed structures require these more physics-based approaches.

Designs are no longer developed with paper and pencil but rather with 3D computing codes. Why should fatigue assessment of those designs remain based on techniques which were never intended to work with the current computing abilities? It is foolish to throw away most of the power of finite element to apply classical stress-life.

Using energy scalar values can be highly effective in updating stress-life for use in the finite element age. Experimental data can be much more objectively integrated with finite element analyses when net section stress, uniform stress, and concentration factors are not required to select test data. Stress concentration factors may be easily determined for many simplified test article configurations but are often not straightforward when based on finite element output. Finite element opens up the opportunity to extract much more information; that information should never be lost in an attempt to retain methods which were never envisioned to fully utilize finite element information.

Energy is a highly physics-based value that can be much more easily combined with finite element in stress-life type analysis. Currently, all fatigue analysis techniques require some form of adjustment. Energy provides a form of adjustment that does not require stress concentration, notch sensitivity, and size effect.

Energy methods combined with improved finite element and updated testing standards can lead to a unification of fracture mechanics with stress-life to provide a much more holistic cyclic loading assessment (Urban).

Unlike the stress function itself, stress-life is a point solution, not a continuous function over the entire volume of a part. Any and all stress-life or energy-life calculations must be point solutions.

Stress is not the primary driver of cyclic load damage. Energy is a more physics-based direct value in the calculation of damage. Using energy-life in lieu of stress-life will provide a clearer, more objective physics-based approach that can effectively unify finite element, energy-life testing, and fracture mechanics.

A general formulation of an energy impact decay function was presented. Determining the details of that function can be done for many materials using existing published data. Combing data with highly physics-based criterion will provide a very holistic approach for uniting key technologies. The elimination of subjective inputs enhances the use of finite elements in determining cyclically loading fatigue lives.

CHAPTER 4

Unification

Uniting Stress-Life and Fracture Mechanics

4.0 Uniting Fracture Mechanics and Stress-Life

The outcome of cyclic loading is not dependent on the methodology utilized to predict it. Therefore, all viable methods should be able to predict similar outcomes within reasonable scatter.

4.1 Uniting Methodologies

Fracture mechanics offers much more in-depth knowledge of fatigue damage than classic stress-life. Crack growth rates, history effects, and residual static strength can be calculated with fracture mechanics. Classical stress-life merely offers cycles to failure under elastic loading. The question is, Which code is most applicable for a given situation?

Fracture mechanics is often presented as a much more physics-based and objective approach than classical stress-life. The only input needed by a user is often an initial crack size. With the initial crack size supplied, the methodology will assess crack growth and determine if there will be growth at all and, if there is growth, the number of cycles to failure.

Classical stress-life has numerous user-supplied inputs. Details including surface finish, size effect, stress concentration factor, and others may be required to assess fatigue performance. The factors are all based on empirical test assessments. Once all inputs are selected and entered, classical stress-life can determine, if damage will occur, the number and, if it will, the cycles to a predetermined fatigue failure point.

Given these general concepts, it appears at first that fracture mechanics is both more objective and informative. This presents fracture mechanics as the clear winner. With only the input of the initial crack size, which is portrayed as a material property, fracture mechanics completely simulates crack growth.

What about the empirical test data showing items such as surface finish being important inputs? The inputs to classical stress-life were a result of trying to match predicted fatigue performance to test results. Clearly, this, at an engineering level, presents hard data that many factors are contributors to fatigue behavior.

Digging a little deeper unveils that many of the classical stress-life adjustments are hidden in the pre-calculation of the fracture mechanic's initial crack size (figure 4.1).

As with classical stress-life, facture mechanics needs to account for results reported in test reports. In many cases, all the factors of classical stress-life remain in fracture mechanics. Initial crack size (A_{init}) is, most times, a function of the same factors applied in classic stress-life methods. Fracture mechanics merely does a better job in marketing itself as objective and holistic.

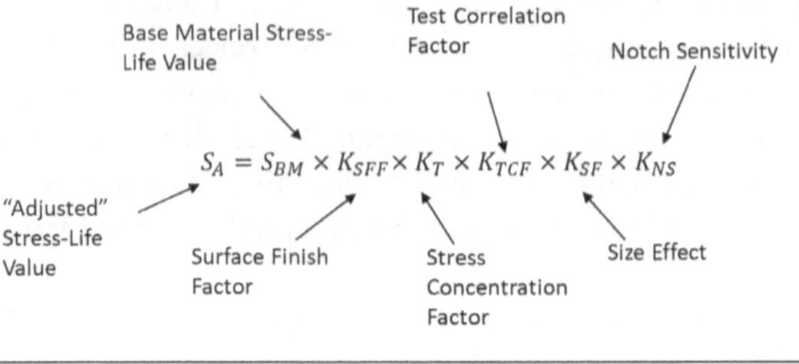

$$S_A = S_{BM} \times K_{SFF} \times K_T \times K_{TCF} \times K_{SF} \times K_{NS}$$

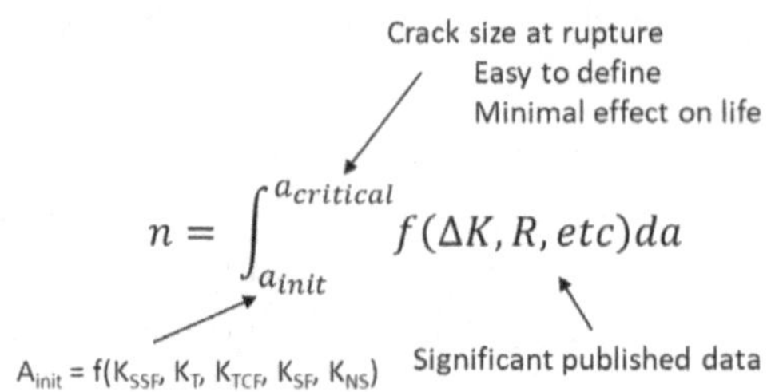

$$n = \int_{a_{init}}^{a_{critical}} f(\Delta K, R, etc)\, da$$

$A_{init} = f(K_{SSF}, K_T, K_{TCF}, K_{SF}, K_{NS})$

Figure 4.1 Correlation factors.

The initial crack size can be very difficult to define in actual design support calculations. Complicating the concern is that many analyses place the initial crack size near a singularity. This means the initial crack size can have a large effect on life predictions. It can produce lives anywhere between one and infinite cycles. The impact of initial crack size is often used as a curve-fitting tool to mask the actual physics of the analysis.

Another issue is the size of the initial crack. Many times, material property initial crack sizes will be tiny when compared to the grain structure of many metallic materials. These relatively tiny cracks are in a size realm where continuum mechanics no longer hold, invalidating some of the very foundational criteria for facture mechanics. Actual small cracks can have features like being non-planar, multisite cracking, and other features not accounted for in the basic theory. This can lead fracture mechanics down the same road as classic-stress life with a highly subjective input (figure 4.2).

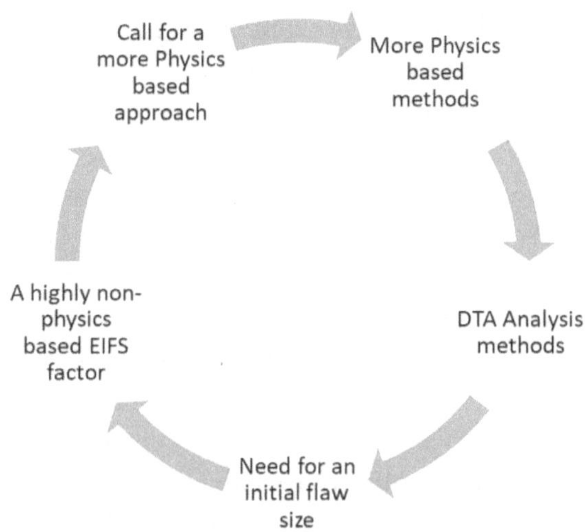

Figure 4.2 Analysis development loop.

What may be a more holistic approach is to enhance and combine classical stress-life and fracture mechanics into a unified fatigue assessment system. The best engineering approach being a combined approach rather than an either-or approach.

4.2 Fracture Mechanic

Many computer routines have been developed to analyze fracture mechanics problems. It's too easy to fall victim to these routines and merely accept their outputs without question. The objective of this work is to spark thought on how to better integrate existing methods to produce a more holistic, controllable, physics-based unified methodology.

Fracture mechanics based on Paris's law crack growth is a very power tool. It's a tool based on a stress intensity factor (K) derived in the William's solution. Which, at its core, is based on an elasticity solution of a single crack tip in a continuum?

Fracture mechanics is a tool which utilizes energy to assess new surface formation for a growing crack under cyclic loading. It is a very good tool at simulating progressive cyclic loading crack growth.

What fracture mechanics is not so good at is predicting the impact of cyclic loading at scales which are far too small to produce meaningful stress field calculations. Without a clearly defined crack tip, stress field, and displacement field, the very foundations of fracture mechanics break down.

Crack growth under constant amplitude cyclic loading will start slowing gradually accelerating as the crack enlarges. If starting with undamaged material, many of the total cycles to failure occur when a crack is very small. The problem for many users is the small number of cycles which are addressed once all the conditions of fracture mechanics are truly satisfied. To account for the majority of cycles in most industry analyses, the initial crack size needs to be so small as to invalidate the objectivity calculation.

This is where the fields of metallurgy and design engineering start to intertwine. In many engineering calculations, the crack is within the grains. Terms like intergranular and transgranular are used. There may even be multiple cracks which have not coalesced together. This is not the scale where design engineers should be looking for growth calculations. It is extremely important to the metallurgist but not a designer seeking growth simulations.

In early cyclic loading, damage may not have coalesced into a single dominant crack. The damage is also of a scale where continuum mechanics does not hold. So why would it be expected that fracture mechanics would apply?

A common way many authors get around this conundrum is to merely assume a crack size. The assumed initial crack size in not a true crack; it is a fabricated value needed to match a test result. The crack has no physical meaning; it's a fallout of needing to match test data. The single adjustment factor (initial crack size) is varied until a single prediction (total cycles to failure) is matched.

Success is announced once total cycles to failure is matched. Most times, no attempt is made to match calculated crack growth with size versus loading cycles data. Sometimes the data does not exist, and other times it is ignored. Under these assumptions, fracture mechanics is reduced to an empirically fit equation that only produces cycles to failure. At this point, fracture mechanics is starting to sound a lot like classical stress-life; only now, there is much more of a perception of physics-based calculations.

This sleight of hand to use fracture mechanics methods to perform classical stress-life calculations can be very convincing. The issue of using an assumed crack size is addressed with nomenclature. The assumed crack length is called an equivalent crack length. Equivalent is better said than calling it an assumed crack length needed to match testing results. The assumption being that the theory and software are rock-solid; therefore, the initial crack size can be precisely backed out of the software.

The equivalent crack length process is bolstered by the presents of a mathematical singularity. The very nature of the predicted crack length allows for seemly minute adjustments in initial crack length to explain a wide variation in testing results. The conundrum is that same singularity that easily produced a wide range of predicted lives for minute crack length adjustments, when run in reverse, produces significant scatter in life predictions. Unfortunately, the latter is done to support actual product design development.

The use of an equivalent initial crack allows all the factors of classical stress-life to be combined into the equivalent initial crack. This allows the fracture mechanics part of the calculation to appear straightforward. While the fracture mechanics appears controlled, the user should be very aware and cognizant of what went into the initial crack length determination.

Extending the application of fracture mechanics to regions where its basic foundation is violated destroys the solid science that the theory was intended to provide. While enticing to broaden the use of fracture mechanics to encompass all cyclic damage, it is ill advised to use it when it doesn't fully apply.

The use of fracture mechanics should be kept to the regions where it applies. Scatter and subjective factors can be greatly controlled when two criteria are maintained: 1) there is a single dominate crack and 2) the scale of the crack size is such that continuum mechanics holds.

Fracture mechanics is a very powerful tool when properly applied. The ability to accurately simulate crack growth is a very useful feature of fracture mechanics. It is this primary feature that gives fracture mechanics the advantage over classical stress-life.

4.3 Classical Stress-Life

Classical stress-life is often portrayed as the older, outdated, inferior methodology to fracture mechanics. In many ways, that is correct, but classical stress-life is very good at what it does. It can plot failure versus number of applied cyclic loading factors.

As previously discussed, fracture mechanics from a design engineering point of view is often degraded to only predicting cycles to a given failure criterion. In these cases, fracture mechanics is not much different than classical stress-life. If fracture mechanics can only relate failure to a given number of loading cycles given an empirically fit factor, then it is postulated that it is not only not much different but identical to classical stress-life.

Instead of competing classical stress-life against fracture mechanics, it is postulated that a combination of enhanced classical stress-life with actual fracture mechanics can produce the most physics-based holistic methodology for simulating cyclic loading and predicting its impact on structures.

One significant obstacle to unifying fracture mechanics and classical stress-life is that they are based on different criterion. While fracture mechanics grows cracks based on surface energy around a crack, classical stress-life assesses cyclic loads using a net section stress. Switching from classical stress-life to energy-life allows the two methods to be more easily united.

Having two methods both based on local energy fields creates a much more easily unified system. Energy-life is used to address cyclic loading cumulative damage when damage is small and not characterized by a single crack (figure 4.3). At this scale the material is damaged through slip bands, intergranular and transgranular damage, along with other microscale material degradation. Eventually the degradation will produce a clear dominate crack of sufficient size to fit all fracture mechanics criteria. The crack will be clearly discernable and large relative to the grain structure.

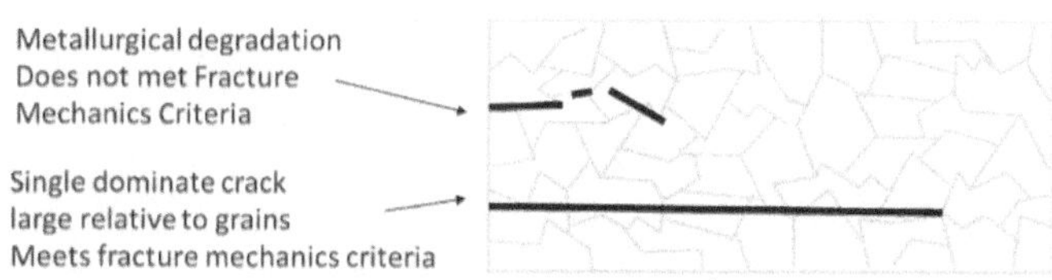

Figure 4.3 Intergranular cracking.

General material degradation with no clear macroscale feature is a situation where energy-life or classical stress-life tools are strong. When fracture mechanics principles break down and crack sizes are of the order of magnitude of metallic granular features, stress and energy-life may be the best tools currently available for generally elastic cyclic loading conditions.

Once a crack has formed, fracture mechanics is an excellent tool for characterizing its growth. The crack may grow and arrest, or grow to failure. Growth to failure or arrest is often dependent on whether load- or displacement-controlled conditions exist. Load control often ends in rupture where displacement control has crack arrest in most situations. In any case, a crack of sufficient size is the perfect situation for applying fracture mechanics.

4.4 Unite with New Curves

Most classical stress-life data is recorded as cycles to failure verse cyclic loading level. The principal concern is with how failure is defined. This clarification was not deemed highly important in many previous works, as crack growth can be rapid in load control testing once a crack reaches a significant size. Defining significant size is a highly variable task which is determined by testing configuration, component material, and geometry.

To improve unification of energy-life and fracture mechanics methods, the definition of failure needs to be tightly controlled. Energy-life curves need to record failure once a definable single crack is detected (figure 4.4). The crack length should be as small as possible for generic material properties.

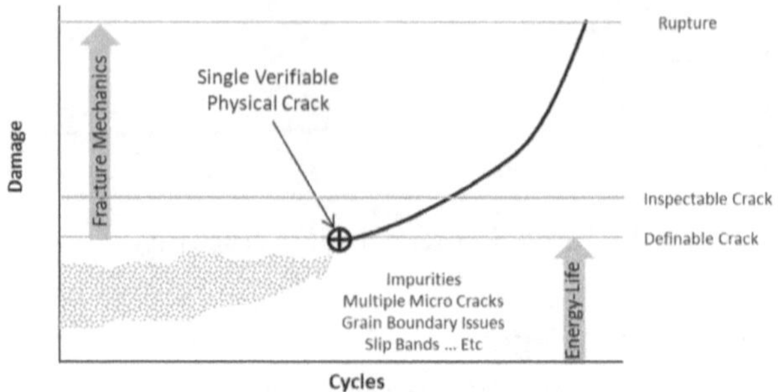

Figure 4.4 Crack initiation.

In general, the crack size defining failure should be as small as the physics allows. There are unique design configurations where detectable crack size is a given input. In these cases, it may be the detectable crack that defines failure. This is the crack that inspection can reliably detect. If testing budget and time permit, it would be most useful to develop energy-life curves which are based on that specific given crack length. Even if applying inspection criteria, it remains that the crack size be sufficiently large based on material granular structure.

Defining failure at a crack size that cannot be reliably detected is not very useful for fielded systems. This is the distinction of definable versus detectable. In product support, what will be most beneficial is to focus crack growth calculations on crack sizes which are expected to be detectible in fielded systems.

Once energy-life curves are developed, they are used as the initial stage of cyclic life. It is now possible to assess fatigue damage to a definable crack using cyclic energy calculations. Once/if a dominate crack forms, then calculations can be continued using classic fracture mechanics theory. This unification uses energy-life, and fracture mechanics is where they are both most applicable.

4.5 Focus on the Physics and the Possible

Forcing fracture mechanics into a total cyclic damage tool is not the optimized approach. Fracture mechanics is best suited to simulate growth of a single crack through a uniform continuum. Fracture mechanic's ability to mathematically represent crack growth presents a powerful tool. As with any physics tool, it must be powerful when it is backed by data and applied in useful scenarios.

Data is an important component to building an effective fracture mechanics simulation. Crack size and growth need to be part of that data set. If consistent grow data cannot be fully explained by the mathematics, then something needs to be reassessed. Lack of accurate growth predictions points to a shortcoming in the simulation. An imperfection in growth rate modeling can lead to incorrect predictions of cycles to failure.

Useful scenarios is an important concept. Users must always ask themselves: What am I looking for, and what will I do with it when I find it? If all that is needed is information on how many useful cycles of load can be reacted, then fracture mechanics may be more than is needed. If useful cycles under detectable crack length information is needed, then fracture mechanics is the tool to use.

Uniting fracture mechanics with other tools provides the ability to determine pre-single-crack cyclic loading damage prior to the onset of classic crack growth. The division of damage regions will allow improved confidence in both energy-life and fracture mechanics. Energy-life allows for the general summation of energy in a region without the need for an assumed crack size or stress functions applied too near an artificial stress singularity.

Many publications look to compete methodologies against one another to seek a winner. Seeking a single winner is far from a holistic approach to fatigue. It's-this-one-or-the-other philosophy can lead to excessive extrapolation of applicable regions producing far less than scientifically defendable techniques.

One common technique to extrapolate fracture mechanics is the Equivalent Initial Flaw Size (EIFS). EIFS attempts to apply crack growth simulation to the entire cyclic loading spectrum. An issue that quickly arose was that the vast majority of cycles in most situations occur when the proposed crack is tiny. So tiny as to be of the scale of a single metallic grain, sometimes even significantly smaller. Some methodologies vary initial flaw size at such increments as to be absurdly small in order to match test data. At these scales, there is no defendable argument for the validity of applying fracture mechanics. There is also no universally accepted database of crack growth.

It is true that in many post-testing investigations, a crack origin can be identified. An origin is expected and very defendable. The fact that an origin is found should not allow the extrapolation of fracture mechanics to near-atomic level cracking.

The use of an EIFS will, in most simulations, start with an artificially small crack, have the majority of cycles occur when the crack is extremally small, have no defendable growth data, and settle for only predicting total cycles to failure.

An EIFS process can initially be highly encouraging. With minimal adjustments in assumed initial flaw size, a huge array of results can be predicted with great accuracy. Don't be fooled. This great success is a result of a cleaver use of a mathematical singularity. This is a resurfacing of an old classical stress-life deception.

The deception is rotating the graph ninety degrees. Unfortunately, the calculation cannot be so easily altered. In classical stress-life, the plot shows a convergence to an endurance with cycles depicted as the independent variable (typically the horizontal, or x-axis). In practice, it is load/stress that is the independent variable which approaches a singularity. In EIFS, the initial flaw size is treated as the independent variable. This combined with the proximity to a singularity shows minimal scatter in initial flaw size. In practice, cyclic predictions based on loading may show unacceptable scatter.

By selecting very small initial crack sizes and staying near the crack growth threshold (singularity above which crack growth initiates), a highly consistent-looking prediction is obtained based on initial crack. Unfortunately, in actual analysis, it is stress which is known. In this situation, if an initial flaw size is selected, a very large variation on cycles to failure can result with minuscular differences in load. Like with classical stress-life, if a scatter factor were applied to the prediction, it would quickly lose validity.

Applying EIFS can do great harm to fracture mechanics' reputation. Fracture mechanics is a highly useful and powerful tool when properly applied. It has to be remembered that most, if not all, engineering calculations require some level of empirical inputs. Separating initial material damage which does not fit the inputs of fracture mechanics will greatly bolster the accuracy and acceptance of fracture mechanics.

4.6 Conclusion

Fracture mechanics was originally intending to supersede the highly empirically based classical stress-life technique. Fracture mechanics makes cyclic loading predictions more physics-based. In many ways, it has succeeded. But over a half century later, it is still a method under debate. There remains a diverse list of opinions on its use. Why does a method thought to be so physics-based continue to elude general commercial acceptance? Why does classical stress-life continue to be a dominate force in cyclic loading analyses?

A one-or-the-other approach may contribute to the sluggishness of fracture mechanics replacing classical stress-life. Reducing the benefits of fracture mechanics by often disregarding crack growth information, or worse, hiding undefendable crack growth predations does not help fracture mechanics' appeal.

It has been generally accepted that for many actual situations, the majority of cyclic loads occur while getting physical damage initiated. This damage will be at granular or smaller scales. The next phase, where micro cracklets start forming, is another large portion of the total damaging cycle count.

For undamaged material, the number of loading cycles under true crack growth can be small when cycled under load control. There may be even less crack growth loading cycles under displacement-controlled cycling, as cracks may self-arrest. This can make the cyclic crack growth portion of either load or displacement situations small.

In many design configurations, actual loadings may be a combination of load and displacement control. Whether load control, displacement control, or a combination, it may be found that true fracture-mechanics-modelled crack growth makes up a small portion of the total cyclic life. Where crack growth predictions are much more beneficial is in inspection period determination. For inspection periods, growth from a detectable crack to failure is important. Predicting cycles from inspectable crack formation to failure may be fracture mechanics' greatest feature.

The holistic approach methodology advocates how to best unify multiple methods rather than an either-or decision. A holistic unification of theories with fracture mechanics used when its crack growth theory holds and, under applicable conditions combined with energy-life cumulative damage modeling, crack initiation will produce the most accurate and defendable predictions.

Physics is the only way to unite energy-life and fracture mechanics. Strong defendable criteria need to be defined. An interface needs to be incorporated into energy-life allowable damage cumulation curves or surfaces by precisely defined damage accumulation to a crack growth boundary.

Initial damage accumulation can be defined under energy-life. Crack growth is easily modeled with fracture mechanics. For total life simulation, an energy-life fracture mechanic's unification unitizes both technologies. The two failure definitions work seamlessly together.

Improved test data is needed to improve theory unification. Current test monitoring technologies allow for the needed data expansion. The extensive library of existing test data can be modified to quickly get the process started.

Through more physics-based testing and analysis, more universal and accurate predictions will be generated. Current sensing presents an opportunity to make substantial progress in simulations and predicting damage caused by cyclic loadings.

Current computing capabilities provide tremendous computational opportunities. FEM methods provide extraordinary simulations with improved accuracy over older hand analyses, and expanded results over handbook solutions. The same computing software also allows for the creation of GUIs and codes so complex that calculations and their inputs are sufficiently obscured, allowing for superficially impressive computed output. Buyer beware.

A few key takeaways:

- Apply fracture mechanics only when crack growth can be used.
- Use energy to unite methods.
- Small material grain-sized damage is general damage, not cracking.
- Forget EIFS.
- Test data for energy-life needs precise crack size definitions (use sensors).
- Remember continuum assumption of Westiguard, Williams.
- Unite threshold with endurance for small damage.
- This text doesn't address environmental damage or acceleration; don't forget them.
- Metallurgist versus engineer, or micro versus macro: what is the objective?
- What good is crack size knowledge to field support if it's not inspectable?

CHAPTER 5

Test Results

Combining Analysis with Test Results

5.0 Uniting Analysis with Test Results

A key oversight in many analysis techniques is the testing data to analysis interface. Current analyses need to combine analytical methods with material data testing. While this step may often be trivialized, it can have profound influence on designs and support operations.

5.1 Test Data Application

Unifying test data, energy-life/stress-life, and fracture mechanics with zero or minimal subjective adjustment is the gold standard for fatigue analysis. In order to best unify the technologies, the most physics-based approach is required. Miner, in his famous paper, uses work to determine total damage. Building on work or energy is an important step in uniting analysis methods and test.

Energy-based criteria is the best suited to unite test data, fracture mechanics, energy-life, and finite elements. Using physics with an energy-based approach to unify cyclic loading assessment tools will greatly minimize the need for subject adjustments.

Many current methodologies use highly subjective adjustments that are given very scientific names. These adjustments are often brushed off, with most of the attention placed on the determination of stress fields. These often-underemphasized analysis adjustment factors can conceal significant manual manipulation and loss of data fidelity.

Creating a unified holistic analysis system will best serve the fatigue analysis process. It is expected that, given current abilities, some level of non-physics adjustment may be required, but it has to be minimized. It must also be very clearly identified. Never conceal or attempt to downplay the impact that adjustments play on overall results.

Uniting damage nucleation with crack growth is nothing new. It has been tried in varying techniques with varying levels of success. What is often done is to use existing stress-life curves as nucleation cycles and then assume a crack size and continue onward with crack grow. There does not appear to be a uniform consensus on technique.

Some methods build on the stress-life curve cycles adding cycles of crack growth. Others assume a crack size for the reported curves even with none reported. An added concern is the use of stress in one methodology and crack growth energy in the other. Clearly, a more controlled and physics-based approach would be beneficial.

To best unite energy-life with fracture mechanics, there is a need to separate damage nucleation from crack growth with a clearly definable criterion. Figure 5.1 illustrates use of a nucleation curve with post nucleation crack growth cycles added to reach a failure or curve.

The proposed uniting criterion is energy. In the progression, local cyclic strain energy will eventually produce local damage, which has the potential to ultimately produce a crack. The pre-crack damage accumulation is addressed with local strain energy. Once and only once a single dominate crack exists at a given location will fracture mechanics models be used to simulate crack growth.

As with analysis, testing needs to be separated into nucleation energy and crack propagation energy. Testing data will establish the number of cycles required to nucleate a single dominate definable crack. Only cycles to nucleation need to be recorded in this initial phase of cyclic loading damage. Once a crack is formed, crack growth data is gathered for the crack lengths of interest. This testing unification method will generate smooth energy-induced damage uniting fracture mechanics and energy-life testing data. The data will be both defendable and reliable.

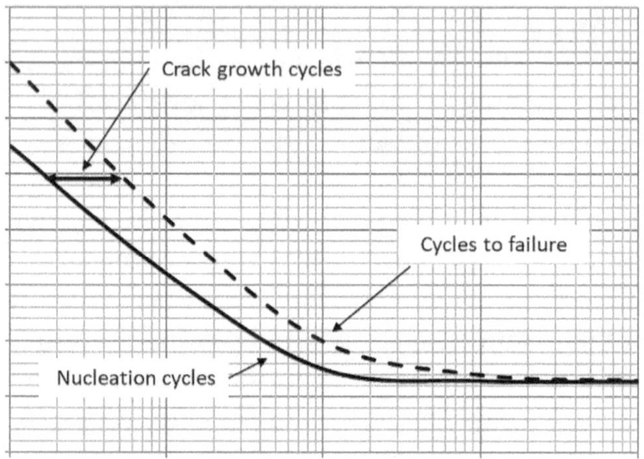

Figure 5.1 Energy in a given volume.

The removal or at least minimalization of subjective inputs will best serve the cyclic loading analysis process. Control and repeatability will be enhanced. Flexibility in design and field support will be maintained. Overall, the process is bettered.

5.2 Energy-Life

Test data has made it very clear that common stress-life factors such as notch shape, size effect, notch sensitivity, surface finish, and others do impact fatigue calculations. Of all the factors, stress concentration has been dominant in obtaining attention. It therefore has been applied to characterize test data for many years, yet all these effects have all been shown through test to affect fatigue performance. As has been discussed, stress concentration may not be the dominate singular characterizing factor.

Size effect and notch sensitivity are both adjustments that were required to aid the use of pure stress concentration since stress concentration on its own proved to be, at best, a trend correlator. The additional adjustments were introduced in an attempt to salvage the use of stress concentration. The larger question is whether stress concentration should be salvaged or abandoned.

Surface finish adjustment has also been applied to help stress concentration as a defining feature. It has long been observed that surface finish with all other factors being held constant has a definable impact on fatigue performance. How it impacts fatigue is still being debated. Should surface finish be added to stress concentration? Surface finish theory was quickly adapted based on observation of the surface roughness. The rougher the surface, the greater the reduction in fatigue lives.

Surface finish effect is greatest at endurance level loadings. This is explained in a similar method to larger geometric features where the higher the cyclic stress, the less impact on fatigue from stress concentrations.

There is a second school of thought on surface finish. It is that the surface appearance merely indicates residual stresses from manufacturing. In this approach, there is no impact on stress concentration. The impact is with steady stress due to an internal residual stress.

Is surface finish a stress concentration adder or mean stress raiser? There is ongoing debate, so how is test data treated and characterized? For reasonable surfaces on quality parts, it may be more of a residual stress impact. While measuring residual stress can be challenging, observing the surface was simple. It is easy to see why in past testing, surface roughness was the clear choice for describing data.

Current technology makes it possible to determine and record surface residual stress. To better unify the components of the process, the internal residual stresses need to be recorded and characterized to fully document test data.

Manufacturing induced surface residual stress can easily be converted into a local strain energy field. The steady energy field can be combined with usage-based energy in a highly objective manner. If a simple correlation between surface finish and residual stress is established, then the use of surface finish roughness, as the input can be maintained.

The unification of analysis and test data can be done with minimal or no subjective inputs once all factors influencing fatigue behavior are converted into stress, then strain energy, and ultimately, nucleation energy. This highly physics-based approach can present a holistic unified analysis that can be both controlled and automated.

What is needed for unification is a single material-based factor. The local strain energy field is what is doing the damage. Therefore, it is the most probable factor. This combined with the proposed distance factor where influence on damage is dependent on the proximity to the nucleation point.

Using strain energy with a distance-based influence factor reduces the subjectivity and number of subjective factors required to characterize test data. The factor is the energy in a volume or area (figure 5.2). The energy-life characterization of test data is possible for all geometries once finite elements are employed. It sounds reasonable that no information should be neglected, yet often extensive finite element results are reduced to a few simple inputs that are subsequently manually manipulated to fit outdated techniques and limited data. It is also noted that most data were never organized in a manner optimized for use with finite-element-generated stress fields.

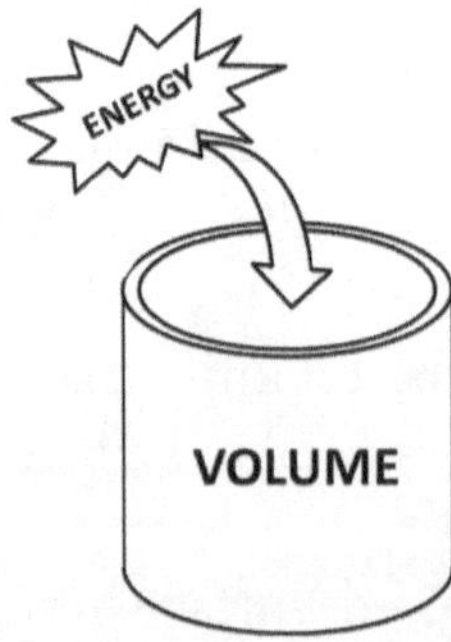

Figure 5.2 Energy in a volume is the driving factor.

Simplifying finite element results and manually fitting a subset of the results to stress-life data cannot optimize the unification of analysis with test data. All of the finite element results must be used with minimal adjustment to fully integrate finite elements and material data. Using the full stress/strain/energy field data calculated by finite elements allows for a more physics-based unification of finite element with test data.

5.3 Fracture Mechanics

Up to this point, the discussion has covered material damage with no clearly definable dominate crack. Early fatigue damage, which most times accounts for the majority of cyclic loading life, will most times not exhibit a single dominate crack.

It may be possible to backtrack and post dict a starting point following a process like the one shown in figure 5.3. A starting point may be clear based on stress field data. It is not obvious when the single dominate crack formed. Backtracking a single crack to a point is not defendable by the theory.

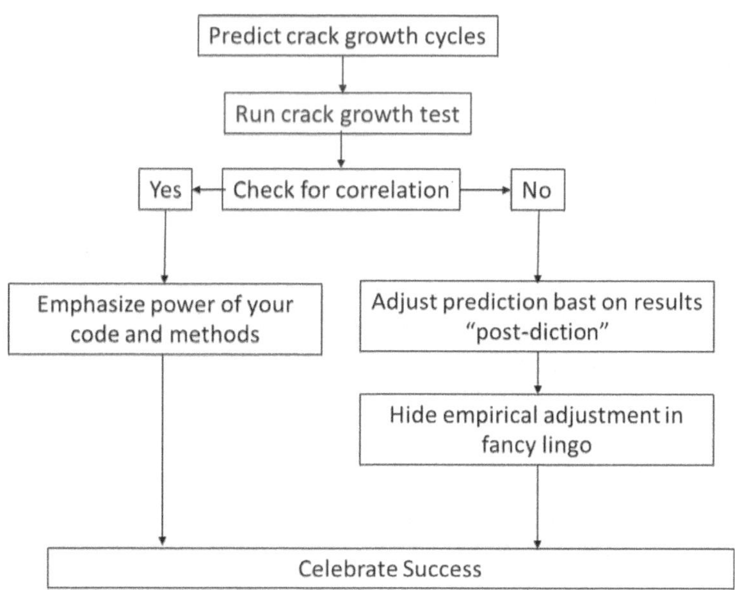

Figure 5.3 Flow chart to declared success.

Pre-fracture-mechanics damage accumulation and fracture-mechanics modeled crack growth need an intersection. To best integrate energy-life curves with fracture mechanics, the energy-life constant life surfaces need greater fidelity. The surfaces cannot merely be identified as failure. Current technologies offer the possibility to add the needed fidelity at a minimal cost. Nucleation curves need to be defined as being from a pristine condition to a predetermined crack size.

Having energy-life curves based on strain-field data with a clearly defined nucleated crack size allows for precise definition of fatigue damage occurring prior to the formation of a clear, single, identifiable crack which is of sufficient size to fulfill all the criteria required for a crack growth analysis. With this added fidelity, the energy-life calculations can be seamlessly integrated with crack growth analysis techniques.

Once a definable crack has formed, it will be advantageous to switch from a stress/strain continuum to a condition where a crack is present. The crack can now be straightforwardly assessed using existing fracture mechanics techniques which are clearly defined in numerous publications.

Switching to fracture mechanics does not relieve concerns with singularities and plasticity. To best unite energy-life with fracture mechanics, they both need to abide by the same rules and regions of applicability.

First, no significant plasticity is allowed for this more typical analysis configuration. If in a more specialize case when plasticity is present, additional considerations will be required. Similar to stress-life methods transitioning into strain life, there are techniques for fracture mechanics to address plasticity.

Second, no prediction can maintain sufficient accuracy near a singularity. Once approaching the growth threshold, fracture mechanics will need to have similar limits to energy-life.

Using similar local finite element data inputs along with like limitations, energy-life can straightforwardly be combined with fracture mechanics. The union of the two analyses can then address a wide variety of configurations and loading conditions with accuracy and consistency.

5.4 Test Data

Testing data from current sensors using laser-based technologies, resistance, computer vision, piezoelectric sensors, and other current sensing technologies can greatly add to the test database. These additional data make for a much more holistic approach to fatigue analysis. Data can be collected as cycles to crack nucleation (Hoeppner). Then when a true fracture mechanics crack is detected, crack length versus cycles data should be recorded.

Limiting initial cycle counts to damage nucleation calculations replaces the use of very small assumed equivalent initial crack sizes. Whether assumed or equivalent merely means the user backed out an initial crack size needed to make an assumed theory match test data. Remember that with a minimal variation in assumed initial crack size, a tremendous range of cycles to failure can be derived. By using actual measured test data and eliminating this non-data value, the analysis can raise awareness to the actual analysis capabilities and greatly reduce scatter in cycles to predicted crack size.

Accurate crack size data versus number of loading cycles is a powerful tool for correlating with and validating analysis theories. By adding crack size, data correlations will be much more robust over only matching total cycles to failure. If a theory does not correlate with total crack growth data from crack nucleation to failure, a deeper investigation is warranted. That investigation can prove to be invaluable in continuous improvements in both testing calibration and analysis techniques.

Moving from artificial initial flaw sizes to measured data will improve predictions and analysis. It will also present challenges in correlating. The challenges are an important part of holistic cyclic loading analysis. In most cases, it will prove impossible to show a perfect correction, which is fine since most accurate, and not perfection, is the objective. In addition to correlation data, a level of confidence or scatter will be created.

Testing with the best available sensing and testing to highly controlled standards will improve unification of testing and analysis. Creating energy-life nucleation values to a prescribed detectable crack size will produce data to better unify energy-life with fracture mechanics. Staying away from excessive plasticity and singularities will reduce scatter and help unification. Being aware of limits and holding to them will significantly help justify predictions. Requiring confidence levels will help to identify unjustified predictions and help foster trust in more reliable predictions.

5.5 Define Scatter

The total scatter between predicted nucleation cycles and the recorded nucleation along with nucleation crack size is a true measure of scatter. After all, it is most important to identify differences between pretest predictions and test findings.

The challenges in these correlations have led some publications to highlight the more palatable small scatter between assumed initial crack size on total life. Once again hiding analysis and testing concerns by staying near a singularity. Only discussing the small scatter of initial crack inputs can be more than just a little misleading. Inputs such as assumed crack size require knowledge of the outcome which will not be known in the design phase.

Often a very small adjustment with minute scatter in the initial, or sometimes called equivalent, crack size is touted as proving a technique. While this could be true, the claim needs to be debated.

A primary question: how did the small variation in assumed initial crack impact predictions? Another question that needs to be addressed: Is the initial flaw size a material property, or does it need adjustment on a case-by-case basis? Remember that small adjustments in assumed initial crack size needed for correlation can be deceiving.

The small differences required in assumed initial crack size needed to match results may only be a factor of their close proximity to a mathematical singularity. This is similar to spaghettification when getting too close to a black hole. When something gets too close to a black hole, the approaching singularity in gravity can produce huge differences in force over very short distances. Where once sufficiently far from the black hole singularity, gravity is more uniform and better-behaved. This illustrates how larger cracks can produce more stable correlations, assuming they are away from a threshold singularity.

The singularity effect appears in small cracks when small differences in assumed length produce huge differences in cycles to failure. Thus, the effect allows for seemly small variations in effective crack length to produce large changes in predicted lives.

A complicating factor is effective crack length. Effective crack length can be impacted with effects of crack closure, crack tip plasticity, or more simply just selecting the desired crack length. It may be a highly subjective factor selected purely to obtain a desired result. Often the "small" required adjustment is shown as a success and justification of the adjustment. What is not discussed is the large change in prediction associated with the "small" input variation.

5.6 Conclusion

Always be fully aware of the benefits and limitations of any predictive tool, or be subject to its errors and possibly faulty predictions. Precise predictions are the gold standard for any analysis. It has become a standing assumption that precise calculations are always possible.

A controlled analysis standard should return reliable, consistent results. While analysis is consistent, physical behavior, whether testing or usage, may not follow an exacting pattern. Sometimes natural scatter will be significant. If the scatter is unavoidable, then a trend may be all that is possible to predict.

It is better to give a more general recommendation when that is all that is possible than to present a seemly precise prediction which is not justified.

Holistic methods combined with the highest level of physics-based factors give the greatest opportunity for reliable, consistent, and confidence in cyclic loading analysis. The holistic approach of combining testing technologies, field experience, computational capabilities, analysis methods, and human ingenuity will generate the highest fidelity cyclic loading predictions.

Applying fundamental physics is paramount in generating the best possible cyclic loading analyses. Eliminating or at least minimizing the use of subjective adjustments is necessary for the highest level of cyclic loading analysis consistency. Energy is proposed as the fundamental factor.

There is a great opportunity, given current technologies, to make significant advances in cyclic loading analysis. The future will offer even greater testing and analysis opportunities. The one thing that will remain constant is the basic physics of cyclic loading.

Be honest with your analysis, and most importantly, be honest with yourself, and great things can be accomplished with fatigue analysis and much more.

- Use laboratory sensors to refine data.
- Sn curve to given crack length.
- Stop FM in a very small crack length.
- After calibration of methods, expand with historical testing for pseudo data.

REFERENCES

This is a list of references that inspired this publication. They include a list of theories, application needs, and data. The reader is encouraged to collect and read these works.

Adibnazari, Saeed, and David W. Hoeppner. 1992. "Study of Fretting Fatigue Crack Nucleation in 7075-T6 Aluminum Alloy." *Wear*.

Adibnazari, Saeed, David W. 1992. Hoeppner. Characteristics of the Fretting Fatigue Damage Threshold. *Wear* 159, no. 1 and 2 (November 1992): 43–46.

Anderson, T. L. 1991. *Fracture Mechanics Fundamentals and Applications*. Florida: CRC Press.

ASTM. 1982. *Materials Evaluation Under Fretting Fatigue Conditions*. Philadelphia: ASTM.

Attia, Mahmoud Helmi. 1992. *Standardization of Fretting Fatigue Test Methods and Equipment*. Philadelphia: ASTM.

Avallone, Eugene A., and Theodore Baumeister III. 1987. *Mark's Standard Handbook for Mechanical Engineers, Ninth Edition*. McGraw-Hill Education. 3–26.

Bannantine, Julie A. 1990. *Fundamentals of Metal Fatigue Analysis*. New Jersey: Prentice Hall.

Barrois, William. 1978. "Stresses and Displacements due to Load Transfer by Fasteners in Structural Assemblies." *Engineering Fracture Mechanics* no. 10 (1978): 115–76.

Broek, D. 1986. *Elementary Engineering Fracture Mechanics, Fourth Edition*. Netherlands: Kluwer Academic Publishers.

Brombolich, L. J. 1973. *Elastic-Plastic Analysis of Stresses Near Fastener Holes*. Presented at AIAA 11th Aerospace Sciences Meeting. 72–252.

Brueggeman, W. C., M. Mayer Jr., and W. H. Smith. 1945. *Axial Fatigue Test at Two Stress Amplitudes of 0.032-Inch 24S-T Sheet Specimens with a Circular Hole*. Massachusetts: NACA.

Brueggeman, William C., and Frederick C. Roop. 1939. *Mechanical Properties of Flush-Riveted Joints*. Massachusetts: NACA.

Collins, J. A. 1993. *Failure of Materials in Mechanical Design, Second Edition*. New York: Wiley.

Crate, Harold, David W. Ochiltree, and Walter T. Graves. 1946. *Effect of Ratio of Rivet Pitch to Rivet Diameter on the Fatigue Strength of Riveted Joints of 24S-T Aluminum-Alloy Sheet*. Massachusetts: NACA.

Dowling, Norman E. 1982. *A Discussion of Methods for Estimating Fatigue Life*. Michigan: SAE International.

Dowling, Norman E. 1987. *A Review of Fatigue Life Prediction Methods*. Passenger Car Meeting and Exposition. Michigan: SAE International.

Dowling, Norman E. 2007. *Mechanical Behavior of Materials Engineering Methods for Deformation, Fracture, and Fatigue, Third Edition*. New Jersey: Prentice Hall.

Eaton I. D., and Holt M. 1951. *Flexural Fatigue Strengths of Riveted Box Beams—Alclad 14S-T6, Alclad 75S-T6, and Various Tempers of Alclad 24S*. Massachusetts: NACA.

Everett, R.A. Jr. 1992. "A Comparison of Fatigue Life Prediction Methodologies for Rotorcraft." *Journal of the American Helicopter Society* (April 1992): 54–60.

ESDU (Engineering Sciences Data Unit). 1990. *Fatigue of Aluminum Alloy Joints with Various Fastener Systems: High Load Transfer*. Data Item 90018. www.IHSmarkit.com.

ESDU (Engineering Sciences Data Unit). 1996. *Fatigue of Bolted Steel Lap Joints and Doublers*. Data Item 96014. www.IHSmarkit.com.

Fawaz, S. A., and Jaap Schijve. 1999. *Fatigue Crack Growth Predictions in Riveted Joints*. Presented at the Second Joint NASA/FAA/DoD Conference on Aging Aircraft Part 2. 437–51.

Furuta S., H. Terada H, and H. Sashikuma. 1997. "Fatigue Strength of Fuselage Joint Structures under Ambient and Corrosive Environment." *Fatigue in New and Aging Aircraft.* 231–49.

Gould, Stephen C., Michael R. Urban, James C. Newman, Shak Ismonov, Michael R. Hill, and J. E. VanDalen. 2011. *Analytical Tools for Residual Stress Enhancement of Rotorcraft Damage Tolerance.* Presented at the American Helicopter Society 67th Annual Forum, May 3–5, 2011. Virginia Beach, Virginia.

Gresnigt, AM, and C. M. Steenhuis. 2000. "Stiffness of Lap Joints with Preloaded Bolts." Presented at Proceedings of the NATO. *NATO Science Series.*

Grover, H. J., W. S Hyler, P. Kuhn, C. B. Landers, and F. M. Howell. 1953. *Axial-Load Fatigue Properties of 24T-S and 75S-T Aluminum Alloy as Determined in Several Laboratories.* Massachusetts: NACA.

Grover, H.J., S.M. Bishop, and L. R. Jackson. 1951. *Axial-Load Fatigue Test on Notched Sheet Specimens of 24S-T3 and 75S-T6 Aluminum Alloys and of SAE 4130 Steel with Stress-Concentration Factors of 2.0 and 4.0.* Massachusetts: NACA.

Grover, H. J., W. S. Hyler, and L. R. Jackson. 1952. *Axial-Load Fatigue Test on Notched Sheet Specimens of 24S-T3 and 75S-T6 Aluminum Alloys and of SAE 4130 Steel with Stress-Concentration Factors of 1.5.* Massachusetts: NACA.

———. 1951. *Axial-Load Fatigue Test on Notched Sheet Specimens of 24S-T3 and 75S-T6 Aluminum Alloys and of SAE 4130 Steel with Stress-Concentration factors of 5.0.* Massachusetts: NACA.

Hardrath, Herbert F., Charles B. Landers, Elmer C. Utley Jr. 1953. *Axial-Load Fatigue Test on Notched and Unnotched Sheet Specimens of 61-T6 Aluminum Alloy, Annealed 347 Stainless Steel, and Heat-Treated 403 Stainless Steel.* Massachusetts: NACA.

Harris, Charles E., Robert S. Piascik, James C. Newman Jr. 2000. *A Practical Engineering Approach to Predicting Fatigue Crack Growth in Riveted Lap Joints.* Massachusetts: NASA

Hartman, A., 1968. *The Influence of Manufacturing Procedures on the Fatigue Life of 2024-T3 Alclad Riveted Single-Lap Joints.*

National Aerospace Laboratory, Netherlands: Nationaal Lucht- en Ruimtevaartlaboratorium.

Hartman, A., and Jaap Schijve. 1969. *The Effect of Secondary Bending on the Fatigue Strength of 2024-T3 Alclad Riveted Joints*. National Aerospace Laboratory, Netherlands: Nationaal Lucht- en Ruimtevaartlaboratorium.

Hartmann, E. C., Holt Marshall, and I. D. Eaton. 1954. *Additional Static and Fatigue Test of High-Strength Aluminum-Alloy Bolted Joints*. Massachusetts: NACA.

Heywood, Roland B. 1962. *Design Against Fatigue of Metals*. New York: Reinhold Publishing Corporation.

Hill, D. A., and D. Nowell. 1994. "Mechanics of Fretting Fatigue." *Wear* (June 1994): 107–113.

Hill, D. A., and D. Nowell. 1994. "Mechanics of Fretting Fatigue." *Wear*.

Hill, D. A., D. Nowell, and A. Sackfield. 1993. *Mechanics of Elastic Contacts*. Netherlands: Elsevier.

Hills, D. A., and D. Nowell. 1993. Mechanisms of Fretting Fatigue. Presented at International Conference on Fretting Fatigue, April 19–22, 1993.

Hoeppner, David W. 1992. "Mechanisms of Fretting Fatigue and their Impact on Test Methods Development," *Standardization of Fretting Fatigue Test Methods and Equipment*. Philadelphia: American Society for Testing and Materials. 23–31.

Hoeppner, David W. 1994. *Mechanisms of Fretting and Fretting Fatigue*. London: Springer Science & Business Media. 3–19.

Hoeppner, David W., and G. L. Goss. 1974. "A Fretting-Fatigue Damage Threshold Concept" 27. *Wear* (January 1974): 61–70.

Holt, Marshall, and I. D. Eaton. 1951. *Effects of Design Details on the Fatigue Strength of 355-T6 Sand-Cast Aluminum Alloy*. Massachusetts: NACA.

Holt, Marshall. 1950. *Results of Shear Fatigue Test of Joints with 3/16-Inch-Diameter 24S-T31 Rivets in 0.064-Inch-Thick Alclad Sheet*. Washington: NASA NTRS.

Hookham, C. R. 1982. Endurance of Riveted Lap Joints (Aluminum Alloy Sheet and Rivets). London: ESDU.

Howard, Darnley M., and Frank C. Smith. 1952. *Fatigue and Static Test of Flush-Riveted Joints.* Massachusetts: NACA.

Huth H. 1986. "Influence of Fastener Flexibility on the Prediction of Load Transfer and Fatigue Life for Multiple-Row Joints." Philadelphia: ASTM.

———. 1986. "Influence of Fastener Flexibility on the Prediction of Load Transfer and Fatigue Life for Multiple-Row Joints." *Fatigue in Mechanically Fastened Composite and Metallic Joints.* Philadelphia: ASTM. 221–50.

———. 1986. *Fatigue in Mechanically Fastened Composite and Metallic Joints.* Philadelphia: ASTM.

Hyler, W. S., H. G. Popp, D. N. Gideon, S. A. Gordon, and H. J. Grover. 1958. *Fatigue Behavior of Aircraft Structural Beams.* Massachusetts: NACA.

Illg, W. 1956. *Fatigue Test on Notched and Unnotched Sheet Specimens of 2024-T3 and 7075-T6 Aluminum Alloys and of SAE 4130 Steel with Special Consideration of the Life range from 2 to 10,000 cycles.* Massachusetts: NACA.

Jackson, L.R., W. M. Wilson, H. F. Moore, and H. J. Grover. 1946. *The Fatigue Characteristics of Bolted Lap Joints of 24S-T Alcalad Sheet Materials.* Massachusetts: NACA.

John M. Barsom J.M. 1977. *Fracture and Fatigue Control in Structures, Applications of Fracture Mechanics.* New Jersey: Prentice Hall.

John M. Potter. 1986. *EDD.* Philadelphia: ASTM, Philadelphia. 221–250.

Johnson, K. L. 1987. *Contact Mechanics.* UK: Cambridge University Press.

Jordan, Eric H., and Michael R. Urban. 1999. *An Approximate Analytical Expression for Elastic Stresses in Flat Punch Problems.* *Wear* 236, no. 1–2, (December 1999): 134–143.

Langdon, Howard H., and Bernard Fried. 1948. *Fatigue of Gusseted Joints.* Massachusetts: NACA.

Levin, L. Ross. 1947. *Effect of Rivet or Bolt Holes on the Ultimate Strength Developed by 24S-T and Alclad 75S-T Sheet in Incomplete Diagonal Tension.* Massachusetts: NACA.

Makkonen, M. "Predicting the Total Fatigue Life in Metals." *International Journal of Fatigue* (July 2009).

McEvily, A. Jr, and Y. S. Shin. 1995. "A Method for the Analysis of the Growth of Short Fatigue Cracks." *Journal of Engineering Materials and Technology* (June 3, 1995).

McEvily, A. Jr., and W. Illg. 1958. *The Rate of Fatigue-Crack Propagation in Two Aluminum Alloys Under Completely Reversed Loading.* Massachusetts: NACA.

Miner, Milton A. 1945. *Cumulative Damage in Fatigue.* Meeting of the Aviation Division of the ASME, A159–164, September 1945.

Moesser, Mark W., David W. Hoeppner, Saeed Adibnazar. 1994. *Literature Review and Preliminary Studies of Fretting and Fretting Fatigue Including Special Applications to Aircraft Joints.* Massachusetts: NACA.

Moore, Thomas K. 1978. *The Influence of Hole Processing and Joint Variables on the Fatigue Life of Shear Joints 1.* Ohio: Wright Air Development Center.

Neuber, Heinz. 1946. *Theory of Notch Stresses: Principals for Exact Stress Calculations.* Michigan: J. W. Edwards.

Newman, J. C., X.R. Wu, S.L. Venneri, and C.G. Li. 1994. *Small-Crack Effects in High-Strength Aluminum Alloys.* Washington: NASA.

Newman, James C. Jr., Charles E. Harris, M. A. James, K. N. Shivakumar. 1997. Fatigue-Life Prediction of Riveted Lap-Splice Joints using Small Crack Theory." *Fatigue in New and Aging Aircraft.* 523–52.

O'Neil, P. H., and R. J. Smith. 1975. *A Short Study of the Effect of a Penetrating Oil on the Fatigue Life of a Riveted Joint.* Farnborough, UK: Royal Aircraft Establishment.

Palmgren A. 1924. *Die Lebensdauer Von Kugellagern Zeitschrift Des Vereins, Deutscher Ingenieure,* 68. 339–341.

Paul, D.A. 1960. *Fatigue Behavior of 2014-T6, 7075-T6 and 7079-T6 Aluminum Alloy Regular Hand Forgings.* Ohio: Wright Air Development Center.

Peterson, Rudolph Earl. 1997. *Peterson's Stress Concentration Factors, Second Edition.* New York: Wiley. 36–40.

Ramadan, H. M., Sherif A. Mourad, Ahmed Atef Rashed, H. Bode. 1998. *Finite Element Modeling and Experimental Testing of Single Shear Bolted Joints.* Civil-Comp Press. 117–24.

Rettew, H. F., and G. Thumin. 1923. *Tests on Riveted Joints in Sheet Duralumin.* Massachusetts: NACA.

Rosenfeld, Samuel J. 1947. *Analytical and Experimental Investigation of Bolted Joints.* Massachusetts: NACA.

Russell, H. W., L. R. Jackson, H. J. Grover, and W. W. Beaver. 1948. *Fatigue Strength and Related Characteristics of Aircraft Joints.* Massachusetts: NACA.

Schutz, D., and Lowak H. 1975. *The Effect of Secondary Bending on the Fatigue Strength of Joints.* UK: RAE Farnborough Hants.

Seliger, V. 1943. *Effect of Rivet Pitch Upon the Fatigue Strength of Single-Row Riveted Joints of 0.025- to 0.025-Inch 24S-T Alclad.* Massachusetts: NACA.

Shin, Y. S., J. C. Iverson, K. S. Kim. 1991. *Experimental Studies on Damping Characteristics of Bolted Joints for Plates and Shells.* Presented at ASME Pressure Vessels and Piping Conference, 113 (1991): 402–8.

Smith, C.R. 1959. *Fatigue Resistant Structures.* California: Air Force Ballistic Missile Division.

Swift, T. 1974. "The Effects of Fastener Flexibility and Stiffener Geometry on the Stress Intensity in Stiffened Cracked Sheet," 419–36. *Prospects of Fracture Mechanics.* Noordhoff International Publishing.

Szolwinski, M. P., Tom N. Farris. 1999. "Linking Riveting Process Parameters to the Fatigue Performance of Riveted Aircraft Structures." *Journal of Aircraft.*

Tate, Manford, and Samuel J. Rosenfeld. 1946. *Preliminary Investigation of the Loads Carried by Individual Bolts in Bolted Joints.* Massachusetts: NACA.

Urban, Michael R. 1999. "Approximation Stresses in 2-D Flat Elastic Contact Fretting Problems." Presented at Fatigue Damage in Structural Materials 2. *International Journal of Fatigue* 21 (September 1999).

Urban, Michael R. 2002. *Fatigue Life Prediction of Riveted Sheet Metal Helicopter Airframe Joints*. Presented at International Conference on Fatigue Damage of Structural Materials IV, September 22–27, 2002. Massachusetts.

Urban, Michael R. 2003. "Analysis of the Fatigue Life of Riveted Sheet Metal Helicopter Airframe Joints." *International Journal of Fatigue* (October 2003): 1013-1026.

Urban, Michael R. 2003. "Analysis of the Fatigue Life of Riveted Sheet Metal Helicopter Airframe Joints." *International Journal of Fatigue* (December 2003).

Urban, Michael R. 2008. *Simple Stress Intensity Factor Method for a Crack from a Cutout Using a Stiffness Modified Shear Only Finite Element Calculation*. Presented at Seventh International Conference on Fatigue Damage of Structural Materials. Massachusetts.

Urban, Michael R. 2009. *Spectrum Loading and Surface Effects in AL7075-T73*. 65th AHS Annual Forum, 2009. Grapevine, Texas.

Urban, Michael R., George Bauer, Thomas G. Meyer, Anindya Ghoshal, Nathaniel Bordick, Gregory Welsh. 2010. *Integrated Statistical Stress Life Analysis Methodology Utilizing Local Stress Fields*. Presented at 66th AHS Annual Forum, May 11–13, 2010. Phoenix, Arizona.

———. 2012. *Integrated Statistical Stress Life Analysis Methodology Utilizing Local Stress Fields*. Presented at 11th International Workshop on Holistic Structural Integrity Process (HOLSIP), February 26, 2012 to March 1, 2012. Salt Lake City, Utah.

Urban, Michael R., Stephen C. Gould, George Bauer, Thomas G. Meyer, Gregory Welsh, Anindya Ghoshal, and Nathaniel Bordick. 2012. *Application of a Local Stress Based Approach in Aluminum Aerospace Joint Design*. Presented at 11th International Workshop on Holistic Structural Integrity Process (HOLSIP), February 26, 2012 to March 1, 2012. Salt Lake City, Utah.

———. Presented at the American Helicopter Society 67th Annual Forum, May 3–5, 2011. Virginia Beach, Virginia.

Waterhouse, R. B., and A. J. Trowsdale. 1991. *Residual Stress and Surface Roughness in Fretting Fatigue.* Presented at International Conference on Frontiers of Tribology. 15–17.

Waterhouse, Robby B. 1972. *Fretting Corrosion.* Netherlands: Elsevier.

Waterhouse, Robby B. 1981. *Fretting Fatigue.* California: Applied Science Publishers.

Weissberg, V., K. Wander, R. Itzhakov. *A New Approach to Load Transfer in Bolted Joints* 1 (1988): 96–101.

Wöhler, A. 1871. *English Abstract in Engineering.* vol. 2: 199.

Wöhler, A. 1855. "Theorie rechteckiger eiserner Brückenbalken mit Gitterwänden und mit Blechwänden." *Zeitschrift für Bauwesen* 5: 121–166.

Wöhler, A. 1867. "Wöhler's Experiments on the Strength of Metals" *Engineering* 4: 160–161.

———. 1870. "Über die Festigkeitsversuche mit Eisen und Stahl," *Zeitschrift für Bauwesen* 20: 73–106.

Zahavi, Eliahu. 1996. *Fatigue Design Life Expectancy of Machine Parts.* New York: CRC Press.

ABOUT THE AUTHOR

Dr. Urban earned his doctorate degree in mechanical engineering from the University of Connecticut. He has over forty years' experience in designing and supporting aerospace structures, serving as a team leader for numerous commercial and military aerospace programs.

Dr. Urban was appointed the chief of structural methods R&D for a major aerospace company. He has published many papers covering numerous structural analysis topics. Dr. Urban was selected to lead the Vertical Lift Consortium's structural technology development program. Additionally, he served on the organizing committee and as a journal editor for the International Conference on Fatigue.